Here is what people are saying about
THE MORNING SIDE OF THE HILL

"In the novel *The Morning Side of the Hill,* a character comments that his restaurant has 'got a menu as diverse as the clientele.' The same could be said of this first work of fiction by Ezra E. Fitz. This love story has a little bit for everyone. Crisp dialogue for any lovers of Elmore Leonard crime novels. A lively New York Latino neighborhood to put one in mind of Junot Díaz's work. And a transcendent ending one might expect from a Graham Greene novel. Mr. Fitz has written a true delight to read, populated with characters you want to follow all the way through to the end."

—Joe Loya, author of
The Man Who Outgrew His Prison Cell: Confessions of a Bank Robber

"*The Morning Side of The Hill* by Ezra E. Fitz is a study in delicious contrasts: it's gritty yet lyrical, heartfelt yet heartbreaking, highbrow yet street-smart. A love letter to Morningside Heights and to Crown Heights and so many places in between, it's a tale of tough decisions, fatal mistakes, the struggle of rebirth, and the immutability of the past. Brimming with enviable depth, elegance, and an intriguing, satisfying ending, it was a pleasure to read."

—Sara Shepard, *New York Times* bestselling author

"Not all writers are created equal or start finding art in air-conditioned workshops. Ezra E. Fitz (now that's a literary name, and it's a real one) started out as a translator and began to write and rewrite books from the inside. In a way, with *The Morning Side Of The Hill* he is still doing that: translating, interpreting, and explaining to the rest of us his story, his hybrid-view of the world, of a New York that's not cool or gentrified. Fitz has created two characters that are totally and completely contemporary masculine: insecure, adrift, broken and incomplete. Ginsburg howled once at how the best minds of his generation were lost to madness. In Fitz twenty-first century, the best minds and souls are eternal

works-in-progress that are lost to indecision, self-doubt and the anxious romantic idea of becoming anything except what they are now."

"There's something of Ishiguro in this novel: it's introspective, brooding, heartrending, yet never pretentious. In the end, an excellent first novel. I wish I had written something like this."

THE MORNING SIDE
OF THE HILL

P.O. Box 4378
Grand Central Station
New York, New York 10163-4378
editor@2leafpress.org
www.2leafpress.org

2LEAF PRESS
is an imprint of the
Intercultural Alliance of Artists & Scholars, Inc. (IAAS),
a NY-based nonprofit 501(c)(3) organization that promotes
multicultural literature and literacy.
www.theiaas.org

Copyright © 2014 by Ezra E. Fitz
Cover Design: Vagabond Beaumont
Photo Credit: Leslie Rodriguez
Book design and layout: Gabrielle David

Library of Congress Control Number: 2014930045

ISBN-13: 978-1-940939-26-1 (Paperback)
ISBN-13: 978-1-940939-27-8 (eBook)

10   9   8   7   6   5   4   3   2   1

Published in the United States of America

First Edition | First Printing

2LEAF PRESS trade distribution is handled by University of Chicago Press / Chicago Distribution Center (www.press.uchicago.edu) 773.702.7010. Titles are also available for corporate, premium, and special sales. Please direct inquiries to the UCP Sales Department, 773.702.7248.

Freydian Disclaimer:

This is a work of fiction inspired by a work of fiction.

With my love to E.E.F. and J.V.F., who are my lanterns,
And my apologies to W.C.F.

The second story within the novel is set in Crown Heights, Brooklyn. Where an ex-convict with a heart of gold meets a young, withered cancer patient whose love of poetry and music becomes their salvation. Together, they find a deep sense of companionship in each other. It's a very simple and elegant story. It succeeds on the primary level: the narrative, the characters, the tension, the conflict; and, for the savvy reader, there is sophisticated magic and mystery on a secondary level.

If these were different times, Ezra Fitz's *The Morning Side of The Hill* might be lauded as an American Classic, a novel to be reckoned with. I fear that as today's reading public consumes mostly entertainment, erotic, and self help books, a young writer like Ezra Fitz is in for a battle. Thanks to the resistance offered by independent presses like 2Leaf Press, interesting, and beautiful literary reflections are still being made available to us. These are the types of books I love, books that may seem so challenging and mysterious that even in the reaching for them, the trying, there's something admirable and ennobling. Books that are trying to tell a good story and at the same time trying to say something human, something that would make Tom Joad smile. This was a journey whose imprint will stay with me, as Ezra Fitz's writes from Mo's perspective, "It seemed so tender, in fact, that he could not bring himself to touch it, and instead he held its image in his mind so tightly that now it had become more than a memory: it was a remedy against the slow and inexorable passage of time and the pain of broken things left in its wake."

—Ernesto Quinoñes

With my love to E.E.F. and J.V.F., who are my lanterns,
And my apologies to W.C.F.

Introduction

IKE WILLIAM FAULKNER'S, *If I Forget Thee, Jerusalem,* the original title that Faulkner and not Random House chose for *Wild Palms,* Ezra Fitz's novel unfolds with two parallel stories told in alternating chapters. The first is set in uptown Manhattan where a disillusioned graduate student and a lonely woman unappreciated by her fiancé run off together in a headlong and headstrong pursuit of passion that appears doomed. I was taken by the tone, the romance of this affair between Mo and Marty, and it triggered many feelings of love and wanderlust that novels such as *Razors Edge, The Sheltering Sky, Under The Volcano, On The Road, Tropic of Cancer* ignite. These are novels for a lost and dreamy youth. The passion of the affair is the journey and one needs not go physically anywhere. The lovers in Ezra's New York City's neighborhood of Morning Side Heights become a universe: seeking, achieving, failing, and in the end, burning but reborn.

There are those novels that stay with me, novels whose characters live and breathe aesthetics, characters that believe that in place of church, in place of priests, of nuns, of yogis, of celebrities, there is art, there is culture. So that the museum, the opera house, the jazz club, the library, the zoo, the movies, the poem, mean empowerment, mean beauty and true transcendental activity. It is this philosophy that catapults the love affair, between Mo and his jewelry-making girlfriend Marty, into a passionate, humanist unsentimental education.

The second story within the novel is set in Crown Heights, Brooklyn. Where an ex-convict with a heart of gold meets a young, withered cancer patient whose love of poetry and music becomes their salvation. Together, they find a deep sense of companionship in each other. It's a very simple and elegant story. It succeeds on the primary level: the narrative, the characters, the tension, the conflict; and, for the savvy reader, there is sophisticated magic and mystery on a secondary level.

If these were different times, Ezra Fitz's *The Morning Side of The Hill* might be lauded as an American Classic, a novel to be reckoned with. I fear that as today's reading public consumes mostly entertainment, erotic, and self help books, a young writer like Ezra Fitz is in for a battle. Thanks to the resistance offered by independent presses like 2Leaf Press, interesting, and beautiful literary reflections are still being made available to us. These are the types of books I love, books that may seem so challenging and mysterious that even in the reaching for them, the trying, there's something admirable and ennobling. Books that are trying to tell a good story and at the same time trying to say something human, something that would make Tom Joad smile. This was a journey whose imprint will stay with me, as Ezra Fitz's writes from Mo's perspective, "It seemed so tender, in fact, that he could not bring himself to touch it, and instead he held its image in his mind so tightly that now it had become more than a memory: it was a remedy against the slow and inexorable passage of time and the pain of broken things left in its wake."

—Ernesto Quinoñes

Chi v'ha guidati, o che vi fu lucerna,
uscendo fuor de la profonda notte
che sempre nera fa la valle inferna?

— Dante, *Purgatorio*

The Valley

MO WALKED UP MORNINGSIDE DRIVE counting the number of cars that had been stolen the night before. The sun was rising over East Harlem, which shone like a scattering of copper pennies in the light, and glinting off the little piles of shattered safety glass that lay along the curb next to the empty parking spots. *Four so far. An average night,* he thought. Mo used to walk up this hill nearly every morning during his days as a graduate student who drifted through the hallways of the big, ivy-laced buildings of the University. But that morning he wasn't walking to campus, he was walking towards his car.

The morning was as calm as it was bright, and as he passed the Cathedral Church of Saint John the Divine, Mo could hear the sound of the waterfall spilling down off the sheer schist cliff towards the pond below. There was something defiant in that flow, something about the way the water and gravity could traverse the stern land in a way that the Manhattan street grid was never able to do. That thin strip of natural architecture had always been something of a bulwark between the Ivy League and the streets of Harlem, and Mo was one of the very few people who were able to pass through it as if it were nothing more than a membrane. Back in '68, the University had wanted to collaborate with the city in building a gym there, but the plans sparked protests and were eventually scrapped. The gym was to have two entrances, one on the East side and one on the West side. Combined with the physical geography of the park and the neighborhood demographics, that would have resulted in having one entrance (the West) for the white university crowd and a separate entrance (the East) for Blacks and Latinos from the neighborhood. Interestingly enough, the neighborhood folk were largely in favor of the project, because of what it would add to the community, while the righteous, rebellious students would rather have a fight on their hands than a gym. Bobby Womack hit that note in the early 70s, singing *The family on the other side of town... Would catch hell without a ghetto around.* And as Mo walked along that rampart of a street, in the shadow of the Ivory Tower rising high to his left, with the gleaming East Harlem rooftops down and off to his right, he knew that note still rang true that morning.

Mo also knew his car would be there. It wasn't because he drove some piece of junk (actually, it was a '98 Accord that he'd got at a public auction of seized vehicles up in the South Bronx, where Hondas were popular with the local chop shops because their parts were interchangeable with the more expensive Acura models), but because both he and his car had been recognizable in the neighborhood for a number of years now. And as he walked up the hill towards it, he began to think about what had happened during the most recent of those years. How had he gotten to this point? And would he actually go through with it now? Was he really about to take the next logical step in a long litany of ill-fated decisions and transgressions? Was this it? Was this that one particular moment in a man's life where he finally and irrevocably becomes something wholly different from the person he once was? Mo put the key in the lock and opened the driver's side door. *This isn't me,* he thought to himself. *I'm too old for this, or too young for this, or something. Aren't I? I guess I'll know the answer soon enough. With the morning traffic running the way it is, it'll be two hours, maybe less.* For a moment, he stood there in front of the open car door, wondering distractedly whether anybody was watching him from up in one of those high rise buildings and listening to the distant waterfall and the clashing of tree leaves in the late summer breeze. Then he pulled off his jacket and tossed it into the passenger seat before he settled down behind the wheel, shut the door, and jammed his key into the ignition. *Well, let's find out,* he thought, and stirred the engine to life.

Mo pulled out of his spot and turned uptown, accelerating past the glittering little piles of safety glass. He turned left at the old jazz club on

125th Street, and then immediately made a right onto Broadway. Eleven blocks, six cabs, and one red light later, he realized that he hadn't turned on either the radio or the air conditioning. Caught between the revolutions of the engine and the questions in his head, he focused on the questions. *People try to leave things behind them all the time. Broken marriages, broken laws, broken lives . . . anything,* he thought. Mo often talked to himself like this, for solitary thought brought him peace like a dog does to an old man. *I fell in love with her. That was when it all went to shit. I fell in love with her and so of course I trusted her and now look where it got me. I'm alone in my car, heading uptown, on my way to . . . fuck.* He leaned over the steering wheel and looked to the East. The sun was a bit higher now, brighter, less smoldering, and the clouds did not move in the sky. *It's going to be a fucking scorcher today,* he thought, and cranked the A/C up to high. He didn't have air conditioning in his apartment, having to resort to a few strategically placed area fans. Manhattan's concrete canyons became like blast chillers in the winter, but in the summer months they were more like a convection oven. *I guess that's at least one good reason to be in the car today.*

Eventually Mo passed the University's Medical School, which was in the neighborhood he had grown up in. Now, everybody between the ages of twenty and fifty claims they went to high school there with Manny Ramirez. But it wasn't Manny he was thinking of that day. *Marty, shit . . . She really did look pretty with her hair wet, though. But I should have known, I should have known, I should have known better. Maybe it was more instinct than intelligence with her; maybe I thought that the closer I got to her, the closer I would be to parting the veil and finally seeing the truth . . . her truth . . . But I know it now. I might not understand it, but I know it. And I'm not blinded anymore. I'm a broken mess, I'm terrified, but at least I'm not blind. And whatever her hatreds might be, I wouldn't wish this on her. Not even she deserves this kind of shit.* He shook his head at that last thought. He wasn't denying it; rather, he was simply trying to call a halt to the reminiscence before it got any more painful. There were no more tears left to shed—they had been exhausted long ago—but that didn't mean the knife wasn't still jammed in his guts, or that his throat didn't still tighten just a little bit at the first hint of memory. Mo turned and looked at his jacket laying there in the passenger side seat. *Is the bulge in the pocket really that obvious? Or am I just being paranoid? Shit, it doesn't really matter at this point. It's all a crapshoot from here. And we're rolling now.*

Up ahead of him, the bare steel towers of the George Washington Bridge were looming in the sky. Beneath them lay the Hudson River, and beyond that, New Jersey.◆

The Lantern

WILLIE WAS PAROLED the same year Katrina hit. He was over a thousand miles away when it happened, but the recovery efforts of many gulf coast cons did not go unnoticed by the New Jersey governor. One story in particular had caught his attention: that of a convict who, after being evacuated from his correctional facility in advance of the rising waters, risked his once chance at freedom to rescue a pregnant woman caught in a cypress snag out on the bayou with only a skiff and a splintered plank to paddle with. That rather incredible tale was bolstered by the culmination of a four-year study by the Rutgers University School of Criminal Justice, which found that well-run Community Reentry Initiatives can significantly reduce the recidivism of ex-cons. At least, that was what the study said. Most parole officers, on the other hand, would rather violate a parolee on a technicality than steer him towards something useful like a vocational class. In any case, pursuant to the provisions of N.J.S.A. 2C:45-1. et seq., the State Parole Board approved a conditional release for Willie and placed him under the supervision of Officer Gino Libretti.

Willie was lucky. Officer Libretti was a good cop without the corresponding bad cop partner. A Rutgers grad himself, he considered the study a lesson to be learned. Plus, he seemed to genuinely care about Willie's success. Maybe it was the fact that Willie had earned privileges for good behavior while serving his term, or maybe it was because Libretti had thirty-seven other, more problematic ex-cons to supervise. But whatever the reason, Willie was never concerned when he showed up for unannounced check-ins, which were growing less and less frequent now that Willie had been granted permission to leave New Jersey and return to his home town of New York.

Libretti didn't much mind the extra commute. In fact, it was he who initiated the move. He'd grown up in Crown Heights, Brooklyn, and—along with Seymore Scagnetti, one of his childhood friends from the neighborhood—entered the NYPD Academy. Eventually, Libretti married a girl and moved to Jersey, where he ended up as a parole officer. Officer Scagnetti, his friend, decided to stay in the community, accepting an assignment with the 77th Precinct. They spoke often on the phone, and one day when Seymore mentioned that a diner on Washington Avenue was looking for a short-order cook, Officer Libretti told him he had a good-hearted ex-con looking for a decent, steady job. Which is how, on that morning, Willie found himself sitting in a Brooklyn diner waiting to meet with a parole officer from Jersey.

The diner had been in the neighborhood since the 30's, and still had that old-fashioned look and feel, complete with a soda fountain, festooned with strings of lights and garlands of plastic flowers, and featuring an impossibly cheerful owner named Gus famous for his egg creams and cherry lime rickeys. Willie had just ordered mango walnut pancakes and a glass of orange juice and opened that morning's copy of *The Daily News* when Officer Libretti walked in.

What's in the news, Willie?

Same old shit, officer, just a different day.

Willie folded up the paper as Officer Libretti sat down at the table.

You know what I do?

No sir.

I start with the back page and start working my way through the sports section. By the time I get to the news, I'm done with my coffee and I can toss the paper before I get to the depressing headlines. You should try it sometime.

I don't think it would work too good. I'm a Sox fan, remember?

Damn it, that's right. You're lucky I don't violate you on that fact alone!

Willie smiled. It wasn't easy to joke about going back to prison, but there was something about Officer Libretti's manner that made it seem like that part of his life lay in a dim and distant past. In Willie's estimate, he didn't even look much like a cop. Not with that fleshy, rotund face and heavy eyes that seemed sad even when he smiled. *He looks more like Freddy Heflin than Ray Donlan. Either way, he does look out for me, though. I gotta give him that.*

The waiter came by with Willie's breakfast, and Officer Libretti took that opportunity to order a cup of coffee. Weekday mornings like this tended to be slower; on Sundays, the line for brunch went down the block and around the corner. The coffee came. Officer Libretti tossed in a packet of sugar and a splash of milk. Then he spoke.

So is there anything going on I need to know about?

No sir.

We both know that a lot of coke gets done in restaurant kitchens.

And we both know I'm not into that.

I'm not asking you for any tips. Just asking you to be straight with me. A man's got to be honest. Not just with his P.O., but with himself.

You know my tox screen was clean the day I went in, and it's been clean ever since. We can do the piss test anytime, anywhere.

Officer Libretti flashed him a sad, fat smile. His flattop needed to be cleaned up a bit, and Willie could see white hairs beginning to sprout at his temples.

I know son. I just have to go through the motions.

The two of them continued to chat, more informally now, with topics ranging from military timetables in Iraq and Afghanistan to the phonetic relationship between Yankee Stadium and Yawkey Way. When the coffee and pancakes were gone, they each threw in a few bucks for the check. Then they both got up to leave.

Good seeing you, officer.

Good seeing you too, Willie.

Come by anytime.

Officer Libretti smiled again. They shook hands. Then he got into his unmarked Crown Vic and drove off in the direction of Flatbush Avenue. Willie headed down the street to Prospect Place. It really hadn't been very long since Officer Libretti helped set him up in this neighborhood, and he was still getting used to his new digs. And his relatively muted skin tone wasn't going to be much of a help in that regard. On Eastern Parkway, he would frequently be stopped by black-hatted and gabardine-coated Lubavitchers asking him if he were Jewish. They seemed so wise, understanding, and interested that Willie almost felt sorry to say no. Then there were the joyful West Indian Africans, with their callaloo, oxtail, and their Carnavalesque parades. Sometimes there were surprising patches of common ground between the people, like the young Hasidic reggae singer who lived in the neighborhood. *Jerusalem, if I forget you, fire not gonna come from me tongue,* he wrote. But the Brooklyn Museum was running an exhibit remembering the tenth anniversary of the Crown Heights riots, and there were coals left over from those fiery nights which were still warm in the community. One night, even a plainclothes police officer sitting on the hood of his car stopped him and asked him where he was from. *It's a hell of a thing when both the cops and the neighbors are asking about you. I read somewhere that if you change places often enough over the years, you'll start to forget where you're from. And then, if you decide to settle down somewhere, after enough time has passed, you'll start to forget that you don't belong there. At least, that's what you hope for. Forgetting. Erasure. Oblivion. And with them, a new beginning.*

For the time being, the best Willie could do for himself was to watch Mexican boxers on TV at a Dominican bar down on Franklin Avenue. But for all he knew about the world or his place within it, he might as well have been at a Plains Inn by the railyards outside Des Moines, Iowa.◆

The Valley

WHEN MO MET MARTY, he was a graduate student at the University, and she was a marketing manager for a large, corporate book publisher. The irony was that while Marty had paid in-state tuition to attend a SUNY school and was now establishing herself in a well-paying and enjoyable career, Mo was in debt with student loans that were getting him an Ivy League education but no clear path towards a life he could see himself living. It created a sense of both envy and awe, and that initial compound feeling might have been what he first liked about her. She wasn't just doing something, she was doing something that interested her, and she was doing it well. Mo's condition, on the other hand, might have be best described as a midlife crisis at the ripe old age of twenty-seven.

His father abandoned him at the age of two; his mother was originally from Santo Domingo, but was a senior at George Washington High in upper Manhattan's Washington Heights neighborhood when Mo was born. Every night, she would tell him old Dominican folk tales and read chapters from books that her mother had read to her when she was a child. He was the only child she would ever have, and she loved him as such. She took every cent from the occasional child support checks and set them aside in a sort of under-the-mattress college fund. Eventually, her graces as a mother were confirmed when Mo was accepted to the University. The savings didn't provide for much more than the occasional lager at the local watering hole—let alone a dinner with one of his highly attractive and equally intelligent female class- mates—but then again, there was little time for that. His bookkeeping was as strenuous as that of any Wall Street investment banker, as he worked his way between the dollars in his bank account and the pages of his classroom texts.

All those nights spent listening to his mother read and tell tales must have affected Mo deeply, for in college he planned on not just being a connoisseur of fiction, but a student of it. His plan was to study contemporary Latin American literature, especially writers like Alberto Fuguet, whose stories of fatherless childhoods and turbulent adoles- cences fraught with questions of what it means to be a Chilean-Amer- ican-Latino-Hispanic-Whateverman seemed dedicated specifically to him. And for a while, everything seemed to be coming up rosas. His professors appreciated his enthusiasm, he enjoyed their classes, and he was looking forward to writing a big paper on Spanglish that might end up becoming a Master's thesis. *Could something I learned on the streets really be worth something at a place like this,* he wondered in awe, feeling that peculiar sense of pride that comes more from affirma- tion than self-esteem. All in all, Mo was feeling more secure than he could ever remember being. Until the party, that is.

One of his professors invited him and a few of his fellow first-year classmates over to his apartment for an evening of café y conversación. The professor was a well-known and well-respected Cuban writer and critic, and Mo was thrilled to have found him to be a casual, affable, en- gaging man as well. There in the living room, the conversación ebbed and flowed between Spanish and English, and as the evening eased into night, the café gave way to glasses of Havana Club rum and soda. By the time the Cohíbas had been broken out, the party had spread to the other rooms in the rather large apartment. Mo stood up from his spot on the couch and went off in search of a refill, but when he entered the kitchen, it wasn't a bottle of rum he found himself staring at... it was his professor, there in the far corner, locked in a embrace with one of the students that started at the lips and ended somewhere below the waistline. He whirled around and left, leaving his empty glass on the counter on his way out.

In the days and weeks that followed, Mo learned from some of the older students that such lechery was not entirely uncommon. In fact, the professor had been granted the dishonor of an underhanded nickname, Windows 98, having once been seen cozying up with a student through his office window back in the spring of 1998. Mo was even more unnerved by the fact that he was called before the Dean of Students to testify as to what he had witnessed at the party. After that ordeal, he went back to his dorm room and confronted himself in the bathroom mirror. *Welcome to the University, Mo. Is this what I can expect from this world? From the people I looked up to, who I wanted to learn from? This isn't what I bargained for. This isn't what I bargained for at all.* He rubbed his eyes and looked once again into the mirror. This time, he didn't see himself looking back; what he saw was a weary, enervated man who looked much older than anybody should at twenty-seven. He felt as though he were drifting listlessly and without volition down the surface of a river, while the deeper current of life itself rushed past him without so much as a ripple. *The unreturning stream.* He saw the empty stoops and streetcorners of his childhood vanishing, and with them went the image he had so carefully constructed about what his life as a student at a prestigious university would be. *I thought it would be true, but now I know what is and what isn't. And it won't take another year or another five years to know this: that I will never again need or even want to believe it.*

After that, Mo began spending more time at the local watering hole, usually dropping in after happy hour, when the bar was less crowded and people could talk. The Lion's Den, on the corner of 109th and Amsterdam, was always full of people whom he understood—whom he felt closer to—than the academic types up on campus. It was mostly neighborhood folks who drank there, since very few students ever ventured South of 110th Street. Sometimes, Mo would stand on the corner outside the bar, smoking a cigarette, and look at the Irish pub just two blocks to the North, which was always packed, sardine-like, with students. *Two city blocks, two different worlds. Just like Bobby Womack said. 110th Street is a hell of a tester.*

It was on one such night that Mo entered the bar to the familiar sounds of glasses clinking glasses, darts hitting corkboard, and barstools scraping across the bare concrete floor. It was a smallish, one-room job with a booth in the front window and tables and chairs in the back. Between them sat the somewhat jagged L-shaped bar and a tiny, sequestered kitchen. The exposed brick walls were adorned with an intriguing mixture of sports mementos and comic book memorabilia, and heavy doors exited onto both 109th Street and Amsterdam Avenue.

Maybe half a dozen people were seated at the bar, and another hand-ful were clustered around a table in the back. It was there, from across the room, someone called out to him.

My man, Big Mo! What's happening?

Mo slapped hands with his friend, Ozone.

Everything is everything.

Man, you look like you just came from a fucking funeral. JJ get this man a beer!

JJ, the bartender, who was also known by some of the regulars as Dos Jotas, grabbed a clean glass and filled it with Mo's favorite lager. What's up Mo? he said as he set it down in front of him.

Mo took a deep pull from his glass, and as his eyes finally adjusted to the dusky light of the bar, he noticed Ozone had some people with him who Mo didn't recognize.

Everyone, this is Big Mo. Big Mo, this is Junior and Marty. They've already met Mike, Hook, Black Jay, and Fabian.

Each nodded in turn, but Mo only noticed Marty. When she looked up at him, there was a searching in her eyes. Mo was sure that he'd never seen her there before, but no further introductions had been of-fered. He sat down at the table with the others, but when they picked up the threads of their conversation, Mo wasn't listening. He feigned distraction, rereading old text messages on his phone, but in fact he was more than a bit taken by that look. Eventually he shook his head and stood up, still holding his glass, and walked over to the bar. He was about to ask JJ who Marty was (and maybe this Junior character, too) when out of nowhere, she appeared at his side, speaking.

That was a little rude of you, don't you think?

Mo turned. She was a good deal shorter than he, dressed in a red-flowered summer dress over a pair of well-fitting jeans. The exposed line of her neck, shoulders, and arms was at once powerful and deli-cate, smooth and feminine. She smiled that particular, mischievous smile to which the male of the species is ever susceptible.

Excuse me?

Getting up from the table without offering to bring me back a drink.

Oh. Sorry. I was just...

Marty didn't move, not even her head. She just stood there with her searching eyes and mischievous smile.

Vodka tonic.

As Dos Jotas mixed the drink, she kept on talking.

But don't worry, I'll forgive you. So, Big Mo, what's your real name?

He looked at her again, looked into her dark, bistre-colored eyes set off with a bit of light purple makeup, and told her. She grinned.

And what do you do?

I'm in grad school up at the University. But I don't know; it's not really what I thought it would be.

Ah, you're one of those smarty pants guys.

Well, no, I think that's the problem, actually. Anyway, what about you? What do you do?

I make jewelry. For a little boutique shop in the East Village. That's my fiancé James over there. But everyone calls him Junior.

By now, Dos Jotas had set their drinks down on the bar in front of them. Marty took a sip of hers and thanked him for the drink with a sarcastic wink, and returned to the table. Mo shook his head and walked around to the opposite side of the bar where he sat down and turned his attention to the late Mets game being broadcast on one of the bar's many flat screen TVs.

Later—it was after midnight, and the place was considerably more crowded than it had been before—Mo stepped outside the bar for a smoke.

Well this is a coincidence!

He turned to see that Marty was also outside, cigarette in hand.

Or maybe it's fate, she added, smiling, her eyes lively. Mo changed the subject.

So tell me about this jewelry thing.

I just like making pretty things. Necklaces and bracelets, mostly. Big ones, pieces that have some weight to them, some heft, but that are still delicate in a way. I like to use scrapped aircraft aluminum; it looks like silver if you brush and polish it right, but it's cheap and easy to work with. It's good for making things that you don't forget about when you're wearing it. Things that have a bit of permanence to them, things that last. Look at this...

She lifted her chin to show off her necklace, forcing Mo to lean down in close. It was a thick, silvery, fang-shaped piece hanging from a length of beading wire.

It reminds me that sometimes you have to fight tooth and nail for what you want, she explained.

It's beautiful.

So, will you have dinner with me tomorrow night?

You mean you and Junior?

No, I mean you and me. Junior's playing with his silly little band at some rat house dive out in Queens.

And you're not going?

Please.

Well then. So where are we going?

You, mister, are coming to my apartment. 228 Avenue B. Just buzz me at seven, my name's on the door. Okay?

Their cigarettes were smoked down to the filters when the door opened and Junior stepped out onto the street. He nodded at them both.

Babe, I paid the tab. You ready to go?

I guess. Well, it was nice meeting you, Mo.

You too. Later guys.

The two of them walked off, heading for the 1/9 train on Broadway, and for some reason, as Mo watched them go, the one detail that lingered in his mind was her purple eye shadow.

The next evening found him walking through the East Village, past St. Marks Bookshop on 3rd, past the intimate, elegant, upstairs Angel's Share on Styuvesant, and eventually past Tompkins Square Park and on into Loisaida. 228 Avenue B turned out to be a fairly good-looking (even from the outside) 5-floor walkup, and as Mo hit the buzzer, he wondered what kind of a scrap metal jewelry artist could afford rent there. Marty must have anticipated his suspicion, because the first thing she said when she opened her apartment door was,

Listen, I lied to you. I don't design jewelry for a boutique. I just shop at one. I'm really just a marketing manager for a publishing company. It's just... you didn't strike me as the kind of guy who would notice a girl who just works in an office all day.

You gave me a line?

Yes but I forgave you for not ordering me a drink, remember? So forgive me for this and we're even. Anyway, come in already.

Mo did, and took in his new surroundings. The apartment was indeed attractive, with a large room encompassing the kitchen, a dinner table, and a living room, and each wall had been painted a different color with what appeared to be sponges instead of brushes. Off that space was a bedroom (which he didn't look in) and a bathroom (which he did). Surprisingly enough, it somehow contained a rather large, freestanding Japanese soaking tub.

It's strange, I know... I have this thing about water. I love being in it. I grew up in Long Island and my dad took me to the beach all the time. Once he took me even though I had pneumonia. And Lake George is one of my favorite places, especially in the off season when it's just so peaceful and beautiful. Anyway, sit down.

Mo sat down at the dining table. On the other side of the thin counter, burgers were sizzling on a Foreman grill. Marty continued to do most of the talking while they ate; asking him about everything from what his own apartment looked like to why he was disgusted with school. As the night went on, Mo began to relax a bit, and their banter began to flow quite easily. At one point, he asked her if Long Island really had an East Egg and a West Egg like there were in *The Great Gatsby*. Marty laughed out loud.

I was right! You are one of those smarty pants boys. You've never even been to Long Island have you?

I've never been East of Jamaica.

Well then mister, it will have to remain a secret for now.

Mo grinned and checked his watch. It was already ten thirty.

I'd better go.

He placed his hands on the dinner table and stood up to leave, but Marty reached across and placed her hand on top of his. Mo stopped, and for an extended moment of silence, he stared at that hand. Her skin looked as white as a rice paper napkin, and her tiny freckles were like bits of cinnamon scattered across it. Mo felt the blood rushing into his ears, his face.

No. Not yet. Please...

Mo sat back down.

So what do you think?

About what?

About me. I mean, what do you think about me?

I don't think I really know what to think.

But you came here tonight, right? That has to mean something...

Marty sighed and looked down and away. It was the first time she had been at a loss for words all night; it was as if by some magic a veil of shyness and uncertainty had suddenly drifted across her face. *She knows what she's trying to say, she just doesn't know how to do it,* Mo thought. *And it's not about sex. She's not the type who would hesitate to bring it up... that much I'm sure of. So what is it then? What is she getting at? What is it that she needs?* Marty sighed again and looked up—not at him, though; rather, the ceiling—and Mo had the vague and distant notion that it was physically quite difficult to look up and look subdued at the same time. And as if on cue, she finally spoke.

I was just wondering what you think about how I look.

I think you're beautiful.

Instantly, Marty's eyes snapped back to meet Mo's gaze. She seemed genuinely astonished by his answer, which astonished Mo even more.

Tonight? You do?

Tonight, yes. But last night too. I mean, when I first saw you sitting there at the table. You were beautiful then, too.

Marty whispered something so softly that it was little more than an exhalation. Mo had no idea what it was, so he staggered on into the silent void of her astonishment.

I mean, of course you are. Everyone in that bar was wondering who that woman was. Couldn't you tell?

I thought, maybe, that I could tell... that you were wondering.

How could I not? You're beautiful.

And that was it. Marty slipped off the edge of astonishment and fell for him, right then and there. And as she fell, she opened up again, and everything came tumbling out. She told him how they had gotten engaged when she became pregnant, about how she lost the baby a week after her first ultrasound scan, about how her fiancé stopped talking to her after that, about how he felt entitled to sex without value, to a life without loss, about how little he actually knew about her without being told, about not noticing her in any true or meaningful ways. She told him how she felt as if she'd lost her child before she'd ever even had the chance to hold it, how the depression had settled in like a heavy black crow, and how she started to scare it off with the other, equally harmful pain of self-inflicted hunger. And she told him how she now felt something worse than defeat: she felt like she had never actually held any hopes that she was in danger of either winning or losing. Instead, her only pleasures lay in the realm of privacy and loneliness. What she didn't tell him was that—until she dared to ask him whether or not he liked the way she looked—she had forgotten what it was like to fear, and that his answer had rekindled an age-old verity in her heart.

By then, it was approaching one o'clock in the morning. Mo stood up to leave, and this time Marty did not hold him back. She walked behind him down the building stairs, and when they reached the lobby, they turned to face each other again. For a long while, they simply stood there, looking at one another, until Marty reached for his hand and took it in hers. Then Mo spoke.

So what are we going to do about it?

I don't know. We'll just have to wait and see and deal with whatever comes.

They said a few more words, and then Mo opened the door. Their eyes met one last time, and then the heavy steel door swung shut between them. They did not kiss.

For the next few months, whenever her fiancé was out carousing with his brother or his band or whomever, Marty and Mo would go out together. Once, they attended a book release party at The Jewish Museum on the Upper East Side; another night, they caught some stand-up comedy at the Boston Comedy Club down in Greenwich Village. The whole island was their playground, and they began to feel like a couple of grade school kids who had no concerns about either luck or fate. They even set up a regularly scheduled lunch date (Marty always paid, being a working woman with a paycheck and not a student with a stipend) at an old sawdusty burger joint near her office on 23rd Street. And it was at one of those lunches that Marty said, suddenly and unexpectedly,

I told him.

Told him what? About us?

No. That I'm leaving him.

Many months later, as he drove through Washington Heights towards the George Washington bridge, Mo would recall that simple statement as the beginning of his education into the conflicts of the human heart, and the fact that love can be just as transient and delicate and yet so caustic as the ray of sun which falls on hanging flowers instead of rain. Yes. The bleak wind, the bare cliffs, the grey waters of the Hudson... these are the more peaceful, the more eternal things.

But that day, after lunch, they did not part and go their separate ways; instead, they went to the Warwick Hotel, which Marty had taken upon herself to book the day before. They did not look up at the 33 Emery Roth-designed stories dwarfed by the surrounding skyscrapers, nor did they hold hands as they walked in under the grand black and bronze awning flanked by flags, but in the lobby, surrounded by polished Italian emerald marble and glittering crystal chandeliers, Mo realized that he had never been so completely enthralled as he was at that moment, watching her stride up to the desk with confidence, with a sense of belonging, and check in. He examined her the way a translator examines a poem in a foreign tongue, searching for the transcendent renderings of love and lust, of pity and compassion, of grief and suffering, of hope and endurance. But his examination uncovered unexpected distinctions, too: *She's sad. It's as if she is mourning the part of her life which has just now come to a conclusion; as if dignity or pride has finally admitted to the crime of self-delusion.* He followed her to the elevator, still not holding hands, still without speaking, and when the elevator reached their floor, he silently followed her down the hall to their room. When the door closed behind them, Marty turned to him and buried her face in his chest. She began to sob wordlessly, and weakly pounded him with her clenched fists. Mo wrapped his arms around her, pulling her against himself, and said,

Just take it easy... It's all right... Just take it easy...

Gradually her tears subsided, and Marty replaced them with words:

Remember I told you about how I love beautiful jewelry? The kinds of jewelry that are solid and lasting and yet still delicate and lovely? Something you can hold onto; something you can show off and be proud of? That's what I always wanted love to be like. That's how I wanted to be held. But with him, being loved was the same as being invisible. It was cheap and hollow and if it were something that could be dropped it would shatter when it hit the ground. Shatter like a broken heart. I never thought it could feel like this, but the second night I ever saw you I learned that it could be. It could be different, it could be indestructible, it could be priceless...

Mo realized he was still holding her against him, her fists still balled against his chest, and when she finally turned her tear-stained face towards his own, he kissed her. A moment later, she looked yearningly towards the bed. Clothing was pulled off by fumbling fingers, landing at various locations between the door and the bed, so that when they finally lay down together, her marble-white skin was flush against his darker tones. Mo's fingers began to lightly trace their way along the curvature of her neck, reading her freckles as a blind man might read Braille.

I hate my freckles, she whispered.

Sucede que yo prefiero las pecas, Mo murmured.

Marty wondered briefly what that meant, but she didn't bother to ask. The only thing that mattered was that they were lying there together, of one body and of one mind, unanimously.

The next morning, they hugged each other goodbye out on the street, after Mo had hailed her a cab. Marty offered to give him a ride uptown (picking up the fare, of course), but Mo declined, choosing to walk at least a few blocks in the gentle morning sun. The driver sped off in the impatient way that New York cabbies do, and he disappeared into traffic before Mo was able to see if Marty was looking out the rear window back at him. He took in a lungful of air, rubbed his eyes, and began to walk. After passing the heroic bronze statues of José Martí, Simón Bolívar, and José de San Martín on 59th Street, he turned uptown and began the long walk up Central Park West. A few blocks later, his cell rang. It was his friend Kingston from the neighborhood. Mo answered.

Yo, King, what's happening?

Big Mo, I need a favor, mi broder. Where you at?

I'm walking home. Why, what's up?

It ain't nothing. Just meet me outside the bodega on 108th.

I won't be there for like half an hour.

It don't matter, just holler at me when you get close.

Aiight. You got it.

Peace.

Mo hung up his phone, wondering what it could be about. Usually Kingston was the guy whom other people went to when they needed something. He worked a few square blocks around his apartment on 107th and Amsterdam, which was known as "the getting place," because Kingston was the guy in the neighborhood who could get you almost anything, from a girl to a gram to a gun. Still a young man, he had done nine years of a manslaughter charge for killing the man who raped his sister, and now he was the very fine father of a lovely four-year old girl. He had the vivid duality of character that was lacking in so many of the novels Mo had to read for his classes, and he often thought that something should be done about that. He was also someone not to be taken lightly, and the fact that he was calling Mo for a favor was as less a sign of friendly affection than it was a sign of serious trust.

Mo eventually passed the tall, medieval-looking spires of the old New York Cancer Hospital and made a left onto 108th Street. A block later, he could see Kingston standing on the corner outside the bodega, exactly as advertised. They slapped hands and hugged. Mo spoke.

What you need, broder?

Let's go upstairs first.

Mo unlocked his building's outer door, and he and Kingston stepped into the foyer. Mailboxes to the left, a framed vintage liquor poster to the right, with stairs and an elevator straight ahead. Mo hit the button. Once they reached the fifth floor, they stepped out, and Mo unlocked and opened his apartment door. The apartment was huge (it was a University-owned building) though sparsely furnished. The kitchen and the living room were combined in one large open space defined by a Velveeta-colored couch, a banged up coffee table, and a second hand TV on one side and a 4-seat dining table on the other. Towards the back were the two bedrooms and the bathroom. Mo turned to Kingston and said

Have a seat, man. What's up?

Kingston shook his head.

This'll just take a second.

He reached down the front of his track pants and pulled out an IMI 9mm Baby Eagle handgun. The slide was locked all the way back, exposing the tip of the barrel and indicating that the gun was empty. Mo examined it, concerned, for a brief moment before Kingston spoke.

I need you to hold onto this for me for a few days. No questions asked.

What if someone other than me decides to ask a question?

If someone you know asks, then you're holding it for a few days because I don't want a motherfucking four-pound in the apartment when my baby girl is visiting. If someone you don't know asks, then fuck that motherfucker. Cool?

Cool.

Here, consider this rent.

Kingston pulled out a thin roll of bills bound with a rubber band and handed them to Mo before continuing.

Yo thank you man. I appreciate it. Give me a call if you need anything. I owe you one.

Kingston left. Mo placed the weapon on his bookcase laboriously, as if it the frame were made of lead instead of steel. Then he laid down on his couch and unwrapped the roll of money. So this is what it's come down to. *You're a human safety deposit box. This is funny. It's fucking hilarious, actually. Making this kind of money by doing dirt and hiding shit from the jakes just a few blocks away from that ivory tower school... scurrying around like a rat along rooftops and fire escapes... it's just insane, man. But it's more than that. It's not just insane. It's a failure. A tragic fucking failure. Unless there's a way to effect something positive from all of this, to bring about the emergence of a grander, more hopeful, more harmonious life from the detritus left behind from the disintegration of a simple, petty, Darwinian world. Yes, that's it. That's how it's gotta be. There's more to it all than simple endurance and survival. There is the need to prevail. To win it all.*

With one hand, he flipped open his cell phone. With the other, he thumbed through the stack of bills.

Listen, Marty. Can you hear me?

Yes? What is it?

Listen, I was just thinking—or maybe I have been for a while, and I didn't realize it until just now—but why don't we take a little road trip. A mini vacation. You know, just get out of the city for a few days. We could even rent a car and drive up to Lake George, if you want.

But you've got classes. And it's not exactly cheap, even this late in the season...

Marty, listen to me.

Yes?

I've got the money.

The next day at noon, the two of them were standing at the Enterprise Rent-A-Car in Spanish Harlem with a couple of suitcases in tow. Marty was wearing a bright red dress, and as he looked at her Mo did not feel even a twinge of nervousness or doubt. In fact, he found himself welling up with an excitement that bordered on fervor and an unexpected yet undeniable faith in the destiny of their love. An instinctual faith, perhaps; the kind of faith a bird has that—when it leaps from its perch and throws itself headlong into the sky and the wind and the ground below—it will return to the safety and security of that perch soon enough. *Yes, love is just a sheer, innate faith in something as light and fragile as a bird's wings.*

Presently they were sitting side by side in the car, Marty behind the wheel, heading North on the FDR Drive. All was quiet in the car; that is, until Mo finally dug up the nerve to ask the question which had been cowering in the back of his mind:

Did he say anything when you left?

He said I could come back. I mean, if I changed my mind...

Really? He lets you go, and then he somehow manages to say that?

I don't know. I think he was trying to make me feel better about it.

No. It's his own suffering that he's trying to address. For the first time in his tiny, self-absorbed world, he knows just how much he's ignored and how much he stands to lose. It was his own, meek way of saying goodbye.

The car was quiet again as they drove through Yonkers. But then, as they neared the long, low, swerving Tappan Zee Bridge, Marty blurted out:

Look at all that water. God I can't wait to get up to the lake and go swimming. To just let the water wash away everything that ever made you feel hurt or angry or overlooked or rejected. Anything that might make you feel anything at all, really.

It leaves you clean and free to let in something new, something better...

Yes, yes.

She reached out with her hand until it found its way into his, and their suddenly awkward fingers laced together in a coincidence of hands.

They were halfway across the bridge, with a mile of water behind them, and a mile of water ahead.◆

The Lantern

EVEN BEFORE THE BELATED SUN began to pour in through his window, a rolling, clattering thunder shook Willie awake. It sounded as impending as an enormous mass of moving water, and there was something guttural to it too, like a deep, rumbling bass line that came and went and came again, offering an undercurrent to the morning's song.

When he stepped outside, a small, middle-aged man known around the neighborhood as The Mayor was sitting on one side of the stoop. He was holding a pint-sized bottle wrapped up in a brown paper bag in his hand, and he chortled heartily when he saw Willie rubbing his bleary eyes.

Dat's him. Dat's de Ole Man! He wake you up!

Clearly, Willie was still getting used to living right next to the above ground shuttle train that ran between the Prospect Park and Fulton Street subway stations.

But you be free now, yes boy! You be free from dat sleep.

Willie nodded at him appreciatively.

Yeah, free. I'll take it.

For a moment, Willie stood there on the stoop, adjusting to the summer's morning light. Directly across the street was an abandoned hospital. Not only was it clearly a pre-war building, but with its shattered windows and crumbling concrete, it looked as if it had endured the Blitz itself. Some years later, as the first whispers of gentrification were beginning to grow louder, it would be renovated and turned into soulless, cookie-cutter condos inhabited by faux hipsters who had no idea they were living in the remains of one of the borough's biggest crack houses. During Willie's tenancy, however, he wasn't too cool to live in Manhattan. He was just too poor. People always say that the world is their oyster. But they always forget that it takes a knife to shuck it. *It just goes to show that they don't really understand the world at all. It's a huge, expansive place, and yet there's something strange and even foreign about every individual piece of it. Like right here. I was born and raised in this city, but here, in this neighborhood, I feel like an immigrant, an expat, some sort of refugee.* Willie stepped out onto the cracked sidewalk and headed left, towards Washington Avenue. From there, he could see the jutting clock tower of the Williamsburg Savings Bank, with the Manhattan skyline in the background. *But it's still New York. And it's still not a place for the faint of heart. It's an awesome city, but it doesn't give you any time for awe. So if you're gonna carve your home out of any little piece of it, you can't drift, you can't wait around, you've gotta act. You've gotta move. And you've gotta find something in and of yourself that's just a little bit larger than life.* He stopped in the diner for breakfast, and turned that last thought over and over in his head until his coffee was cold. *No matter what else, it's good to be back in the City.*

Willie spent much of the rest of the day exploring. At first he walked past huge graffiti murals, stunted trees struggling to grow in little squares of packed dirt and crab grass, and liquor stores where customers shouted out orders to clerks encased in Plexiglas. Later, he strolled down Eastern Parkway, studying the plaques placed at the base of the trees and etched with the names of people who died during The Great War. He walked the circumference of Grand Army Plaza, and he stopped in the Brooklyn Public Library so he could check his email. He had lunch at a Tex Mex joint on Flatbush called Tommy Taco. And after that, he spent the rest of the afternoon pacing up and down the Long Meadow in Prospect Park, thinking over and over again about what he'd done, why he'd done it, and who he'd done it for. *But I think too much. In the past, I had a future. I had a plan. Then again, that was years ago. Now I've got to focus on just living in the present. Stop trying to justify things, to explain them away. Just let them all fade, and think about beginning again. But can you start over at thirty-*

five? *Haven't you crossed some line by that point? But there you go again... too much self-analysis. Things will end up the way they end up, and they'll do it whenever they damn well want to.* But as every man knows, time and the tide wait for no one, and soon it was time for him to return to the diner and begin his nightly shift.

To Willie, it seemed as if there were something illicit in making omelets at night. Perhaps it's just the way a criminal—or even an ex-con like himself—thinks, but even making breakfast after dark seemed like yet another small transgression. But he had worked in kitchens much of his short adult life, and being in one was more familiar than foreign to him. Plus, it felt good to be making money again. *Or rather, it felt good to be allowed to make money again. To be allowed to work for it.* He mopped floors and hauled trash in his college cafeteria, and in the summers he worked for a large catering company. By the time he had arrived at the Brooklyn diner, he was ambidextrous with sauté pans and adept enough to find a sense of peace amidst the controlled, clattering chaos of a fast-moving kitchen. Cooks are a colorful sort, and not just at the Anthony Bourdain level. Tiny Colletto, one of the other cooks who worked at the diner, used to work in the galley of a fishing vessel that patrolled Baja California and the Sea of Cortéz out of San Diego. He adored sea turtles, detested Sally Lightfoots, and was an avid spearfisherman. Every once in awhile, late into their nighttime shift, he would tell Willie stories about his many failed attempts at going after manta rays with a harpoon. Willie hand never gone fishing in either fresh or salt water before, and Tiny, who had taken a liking to his kitchen mate, extended a standing offer to take him out for a day on the Long Island Sound.

Around two in the morning, when the dry storage had been restocked and the walk-in refrigerator was padlocked, Willie changed his shirt, punched his time card, and stepped out into the night. Then a voice called out from behind him. It was Tiny.

Hey Willie, you ain't going home yet, are you?

I was intending to.

Nah, man. Come with me. I know this awesome little joint. It's just a few blocks down from here.

Willie nodded.

I could use a little more exploration.

They walked down Underhill towards Atlantic Avenue. Tiny was wearing a white Navy cap which he claimed he traded for in a San

Diego port, and Willie was still in his baggy, black-and-white checkered chef pants now stiff with rendered grease. This part of the neighborhood was a bit nicer than Willie's spot just a few block to the East, as the street was lined with a new block of row houses instead of barely code-worthy tenement slums. A block later, they stopped in front of The Dean: an idyllic-looking corner tavern flanked by an open-air back patio and ringed by a series of potted plants like palm trees around a desert oasis. The two men entered, and sat down at the massive mahogany bar. They were greeted by the bartender, who introduced himself in a voice that sounded as if it were generated by a V-twin turbo diesel Harley Davidson engine.

My name's Dave. What'll it be for you guys tonight?

They each ordered a pint of Brooklyn Lager.

Willie took a long, slow pull from his glass and examined the interior of the bar. At the far end was the door leading out into the patio, and a short set of stairs leading down into a separate dining room. The bar area itself was empty save for three young men sitting at one of the square, paper-covered tables. On the opposite wall hung an enormous framed Italian film poster. Willie contemplated it for a minute. *Clearly, that's a likeness of Marlon Brando sitting at the table there with a cigarette and a gun, and that's Jane Fonda and Robert Redford there cowering in the background. But what the hell does "La Caccia" mean?*

It's "The Chase."

Willie turned around to see Dave flashing him a gnarled, toothy grin.

Never seen it. Is it any good?

It is if you like that sort of thing. So you boys coming from work tonight?

Yeah, at the diner up Washington Avenue.

Oh yeah, I know that place. I hear they do a mean Sunday brunch. I'd go try it sometime myself, but we do our own brunch here. That's one of our cooks sitting over there with a couple of the regulars around here.

Willie raised his glass to the group, and they nodded in return.

So how 'bout that Syracuse game tonight? That freshman they got looks like the real deal. No way he's sticking around for another season!

Dave growled and grinned and went back to stacking glasses. James Brown's "The Boss" began to ooze out of the barroom speakers, and Willie couldn't help but grin a bit himself. *I guess I've paid a high enough cost. Maybe not enough to be the boss of anything, but enough at least to be able to sit down at a friendly little corner tavern to drink and smile...*

The Dominican bar on Franklin where he went to watch fights was a very different sort of place. The matriarch who owned the small establishment was nice enough, and she liked him because he spoke Spanish. She even had her two sons walk Willie home from time to time until his face became recognizable enough in the neighborhood. *You a good kid, she said, pero nadie te conoce en este barrio. I don't want you getting gaffled en la calle.* But people can be kind and morose at the same time. That fact was never more obvious than the night that Vargas lost to De la Hoya. The regulars had been waiting a long time—years, even—for this fight to happen, but that night, even before the Round 1 bell rang, there was a mournful sort of hopelessness in their kind eyes. The fight had been debated so often leading up to the event that it was as desiccated as an autumn leaf. Each argument both for and against had been made time and time again. *And then I showed up. A stranger, un extranjero, appearing in their familial bar. That stirred them up a little bit. But then they found out I was for Vargas too. There was nothing new there after all. And they quite literally turned away, almost ruminant; they turned their backs to the gloom and huddled over their beers like livestock in the rain.* It was the most dejected little bar that Willie had ever been to, but he was at least tolerated there if not accepted, and Willie went there from time to time for the simple reason of having nothing better to do. The name of the place was "Siempre Amigos," but it might as well have been "Siempre Abatidos." It was the same men every time, short and stocky both in stature and temperament, who spent as much time as possible at the bar, leaving only to eat or sleep before returning again to sit at the bar and wait for fight night to arrive. It was not faith that they had, it was a stoicism, and it hung over them with the permanence of gravity. From time to time, one of them would stand up with a grimace, make his way over to the juke box, and punch in some bachata or merengue. But no matter how loudly it blared out over the speakers, it forced no joy into that tiny place. The bar sold Presidente beer and only Presidente beer, and once, while Elvis Crespo was singing about soft kisses, Willie bought a round of beers, which elicited a muted cheer from the patrons. The matriarch thanked him by mixing a special drink: a margarita made with damiana instead of triple sec.

Estuvo bien hacerlo, she said, leaning across the bar.

Es una canción alegre. Solo pensé que merecía un poco más de alegría. Es todo.

Alegría? No hay mucho de eso aquí.

She went on to tell him how one of the regulars had grown up in Flatbush in the 1950s, watching Roy Campanella, El Duque Snider, and Yaqui Robinson play ball at Ebbets Field. She told him how he would sit in the bleachers and cheer for Los Bums and even boo the great Mays, who played for their rivals, Los Gigantes. And she told him that he no longer believed in Heaven. Fue derrumbado en 1960, he said.

But Willie was at the Dean now, where people ate and drank and simply snorted a bit when great players left town. He and Tiny downed a few more pints of lager before Tiny decided to call it a night. Willie was feeling content and comfortable though, and decided to stay. A few minutes after Tiny left, the cook sitting at the table motioned for him to come and join them.

Dave said you work at the diner up on Washington?

Yeah, though I just started a month or so ago.

That explains why he hasn't seen you before. Don't worry about it, though. People eventually end up finding their way here.

I can see why. You got a pretty sweet thing going on here. I'm sure the menu's better than ours.

We got a menu as diverse as the clientele.

He chuckled a bit.

That's what some reviewer once wrote. You know, combining pub grub with soul food. Fusion cuisine, and all that shit.

He laughed again. Willie did too.

I'm Kenyatta. Kenyatta Blake. This is Dante Smith, and this is Equality Greene.

I'm Willie.

They all shook hands across the table.

So Kenyatta, how did you end up at a classy joint like this? Did you go to culinary school or something?

Nah, man. I'm not a chef, I'm just a cook. This is just a day job, so to speak.

So what's the night gig?

Hip hop, man. It's the love of my life. I built a little studio lab up in my apartment over on Vanderbilt, and the three of us lay down some shit up there on the second floor.

Anything I might have heard of?

We got a single called "Walk the Beat" that's getting some airplay on Medgar Evers' student radio. Equality's mother is an English professor there.

No shit?

Equality nodded. Kenyatta continued providing the background information.

Dante works at the bookstore on Washington.

The one right next to the C-Town?

Dante spoke up.

That's the one. Oldest Black bookstore in Brooklyn.

Man, I walk past it every day, but I've never gone in.

Drop by sometime and pick up a calendar. There's a sick-ass poetry slam every month. Real good stuff.

I will, man. Most definitely.

So what about you, bro? What brings you to the Heights?

Willie knew this point in the conversation had been coming. Other than Officer Libretti, his old friend in the 77th Precinct, and the owner of the diner, nobody knew about his illicit past. He used to be afraid about some elements of his past, but that was before his arrest and conviction, before he entered the correctional facility. And it corrected him, all right. It corrected him through suffering. *It cut me off violently from everything I ever knew (even if I was fleeing from it myself) and tossed me into a place so unpredictable that even the fear felt foreign. I wonder how many sociology studies have been done on that. On the theory that people can be most easily changed when they're fearful, suffering, vulnerable, wounded, defeated. It's the same way you get people to go on daytime TV talk shows and give up their stories. They ask you questions about what you've done, and they either cut you off for good—which is just another way of saying cutting you free—or they forgive you. But there is never an instance of "forgive-and-forget." There is no forgetting. Never.* Willie never liked those kinds of shows, but there was some air of comfort in the confines of this tavern, and he felt relaxed around these newfound neighbors. Perhaps the beer was a help, but Willie was quite certain that nobody in prison had ever called him "bro" without some hint of affectation.

So he told them. Told them everything. And dispassionately, too. He told them about the mistakes he had made, his errors in the fields of both judgment and trust, and about all the time he'd had to review them. At the end of it all, he had come to the realization that it would be better to never have to make those kinds of decisions ever again than it would be to make the right ones. He ended it all simply enough:

Anyway, my P.O. knows a guy in the 77 squad. He got me the job at the diner.

No shit? There's a lot of cops from that squad out on the streets. All in plain wrappers. All types of units, too. Narcotics, anti-crime, cage units, you name it. You'll start to notice 'em, though. Spend enough time on the block and you'll start to notice 'em.

I think I already did.

Willie told them the story about the officer sitting on the hood of his car who questioned him on the street one night.

No shit? What'd he say?

He asked me if I had a gun. I said no. Then he told me I'd better get one, and laughed.

Ah, that sounds like Officer Coffey, for sure. He's a real ball buster. Pinched me once for simple possession.

Equality interrupted his friend, injecting himself into the conversation.

Speaking of which, what'd you go in for, anyway?

Willie told them that part of the story. After all, it's not like he murdered somebody. And he had an excuse. He could use it to play the victim and gain the sympathy of men everywhere.

Kenyatta sucked in his breath through his teeth.

Damn, nigga. Where'd you do your bid?

East Jersey State Pen.

Ain't that a motherfucker! Yo Dave, we need some shots of Patrón over here!

When Dave lined them up, they each took a glass and held it up. Kenyatta provided the toast:

Fuck the State Pen, fuck hoes at Penn State!

When that round was down, they ordered another one. This time, it was Equality who spoke.

Welcome to the neighborhood Willie. No matter where you go, from Bucktown to Uptown, you're always welcome back here. So you know.

They continued to drink there at the tavern until closing time. When they finally left, Kenyatta, Dante and Equality headed West towards Vanderbilt Avenue, and Willie struck out to the East, back to his apartment. He passed chain-link fences sequestering chop shops, and no dogs barked. Even at this time of night, with dawn still more than an hour away, the sky was very light, and the stars were nonexistent. The combination of beer and liquor was warm in his belly, and the night air had a recognizable quality to it, something that felt less alien than it had before. Willie slowed down to an unhurried pace. A block later, he noticed a strange marking on the base of a streetlight. He stopped and bent down to get a closer look at it, and discovered the smallest bit of graffiti that he had ever seen in his life. It covered an area the size of a paperback book, and was designed to look like a United States Postal Service Priority Mail label. In the address space, the following words were written in a sharp yet flowing hand:

The feeble sodium light fell over these words like a halo. There was something very solemn and solitary about this place, and as Willie continued to gaze upon it, he began to slowly realize that it was marking the place where someone had died. He had seen a blue "CGC" tag on a door on the 2/3 train platform at Eastern Parkway, though there was nothing that seemed to be gang-related here. But also missing from the site were any signs that it had been visited by this person's family. *I wonder if he had any. If they took his body and buried it alongside the graves of his relatives. Perhaps not. Perhaps he died indigent and unbefriended and perhaps even unknown. Yes. That's it. He's up there, lying in Potter's Field on Hart Island with no company save for Saint Matthew himself. Cemeteries are for friends and family to visit and reminisce. But for the unnamed dead, the place where the last light of life flashes across his eyes is the only meaningful one, whether it is a nocturnal Brooklyn streetcorner, the grassy dunes outside a tiny Mexican fishing town, or a hotel room by the freeway on a cloudy, gauzy, gray afternoon.*

Willie continued walking on down the street, leaving the tiny, anonymous tribute behind him in the dark like a fictitious memory. When he got back to his building and unlocked the outer door, he heard loud, thundering music coming from the apartment next to his. Curious, he knocked on the door. But even more curious was the fact that a skinny, short-haired, thirty-something girl opened the door.

Oh shit… I'm sorry, did we wake you up?

Uh, no, actually I'm just getting home.

You wanna come in? Have a nightcap with your new next-door neighbor?

She smiled an easy, exhausted, carefree smile and held up the cocktail glass she was holding as if to prove that her offer was sincere. Willie was disarmed. Counting the bartender at the Dean and the three neighborhood patrons, he hadn't met this many friendly people in a day since moving here.

You know what? That actually sounds pretty damn good.

She held the door for him as he walked inside. As he walked past her, he couldn't help but notice that she didn't smell like alcohol. *In fact, she smells like apple blossoms. An entire orchard of apple blossoms.* Her apartment was laid out exactly the same as his was, just a mirror image of it. The music was loud and raucous, if not entirely justified by the scant number of guests still in attendance.

My name is Alba Lucía, by the way. I was supposed to move in on the first, but I had some issues getting packed and getting a truck. So if you were wondering why it looks so empty in here, it's not because I'm going for some sort of "Norwegian Wood" kind of Feng Shui thing here, it's because half of my stuff is still at the Public Storage warehouse over on Utica.

You have a phenomenal name.

Thanks! You know what though? To be honest, I can't stand it myself. It's just got too many syllables.

What do your friends call you?

You mean like a nickname?

Yeah.

My dad used to call me Bita when I was a little girl. You know, short for "Albita?" But other than that, I don't think I've ever had one.

Really? Well, that's something we are gonna have to work on.

Oh? Are we now?

Yeah. I'll help. Like, if you played for the Yankees, they'd probably call you A-Loose.

Somehow that sounds deeply, deeply dirty.

Well, on the simple side of the equation, you could go with A.L. Or even better yet, just Al.

She instantly broke into laughter.

Al? You want to call me Al?

Willie grinned. Then he replied in a mock-serious voice.

Yes. Yes I do.

Well in that case, I guess it's okay by me. So, what can I get you to drink?

Well, Al, I'll take a beer, if you've got one.

In the kitchen. Follow me.

Willie did as he was told. A Styrofoam cooler on the floor was empty, save for some rapidly melting ice. Al opened the refrigerator.

All I have left is some Budweiser.

Which was literally true. The refrigerator was bare, save for a Brita pitcher and a half-empty case of Bud bottles.

That's fine by me.

Willie twisted off the cap and looked around for a garbage can to toss it in. Not finding one, he stuffed it in the back pocket of his checkered kitchen pants and took a sip. Alba Lucía was still holding the drink she'd answered the door with, but she downed it in one fell gulp.

What did you say your name was?

Willie smiled.

I didn't. But that's okay. It's Willie.

So Willie, where are you from?

I'm a New Yorker, born and raised. I've been gone for a few years, though. Just recently moved back to the city. What about you?

I grew up in Jackson Heights, but like I said, I just moved in here a little bit ago myself. So what do you think of the neighborhood so far?

I think I need to get to know it a little bit better.

I agree. Have you been to that club Utopia? It's pretty funny... they only frisk the white people who go there. Everyone thinks they're cops.

I've never been inside, but I've seen the lines outside on the weekends. Tonight I was just at the Dean, over on Underhill.

Oh, yeah. They have an amazing Sunday brunch.

Better than the brunch at the Diner on Washington?

Much. We should go sometime. What do you think?

Willie thought it was a wonderful idea. They talked there, standing in the kitchen, until a lightening of the horizon indicated to them that dawn was near. Then they said their good nights. Back in his room, Willie laid down on his couch and looked up at the slowly rotating blades of the ceiling fan in silence. The morning sun filtered in through the slits in the Venetian blinds, casting slow-moving parallel shadows across his body and the wall behind him. Al had turned off her music; he would be hearing the repeated rumblings of the shuttle train very soon. *It was a good day, and a good night as well. Maybe I'll be seeing more of those in the near future. Sure, the freaks come out at night, and the baseheads will always be out panhandling for crack funds, but there are some decent people around here too. Like Al. It was good to meet her. No, wait... it wasn't just good to meet her. It was fun. I haven't really enjoyed hanging out with someone in a long time. A long time. This building, this neighborhood, it isn't so bad. They say that if you can overcome fear, you can achieve anything. And nothing is more frightening than being alone. That's what people run from. So maybe there's some peace to be made here. Maybe even some friendships.*

Willie wanted to go to sleep on that thought, but his mind wasn't quite willing to permit that just yet. He got up off the couch and walked over to his bookcase, from which he selected a collection of García Lorca's poetry. Some convicts study religion or learn chess when they go into the system. Willie, on the other hand, read poetry. And after idly leafing through the pages for the better part of an hour, he reached to the coffee table for a pen. In the margins of page 224, he rewrote one of the poems:

Hermosita mía
Yo no sé qué tiene
En tu manzanal
Que tan dulce me huele.◆

The Valley

THE MORNING AFTER THEIR FIRST NIGHT on the lake, Mo awoke to find a note for him on the nightstand: *Back soon. Or maybe later. M.* Lacking any prospects for morning sex, Mo rolled over and went back to sleep. He was still asleep on his side when Marty returned sometime around eleven and sat down on the bed next to him. She stroked his hair until he slowly woke up again and looked up into the darkness of her eyes and the brightness of her teeth. *So this is what it's like to feel wholly at peace with the world, to know at once and forever that it's not about jobs or money or college degrees or even sex or marriage... It's about waking up and not feeling cold in the morning, not feeling worry or fear or isolation.* He was surprised, then, by Marty's first words to him that day:

Do you trust me?

Baby, what do you mean?

I mean, do you believe in me? Do you look at me and see someone you could put your trust in? After what I did?

Of course I do...

But how can you say that? How can you really mean that? How would you ever know that I wouldn't do to you what I did to... to him?

She's terrified. In fact, she's so terrified that she doesn't even know what to fear more: being alone, or being unloved.

I do because trust is a choice I made. I choose to trust you, to believe in you. In us. I look at you and honestly, that's the only real choice there is for me to make.

Mo recognized the look that came over Marty's eyes as the same one she wore the first time he told her he thought she was beautiful. *I choose to trust because there's love in those eyes. It's the sort of thing that binds people together along with faith and belief. It's like concrete. You can't walk down the sidewalk if you can't trust the concrete, and you can't move through life if you can't bring yourself to trust love.*

Thank you.

For what?

For holding me together when I feel like falling apart.

It's alright. We're lucky, actually. We both have something we can both hold onto when we need to.

Marty smiled.

I like the sound of that. And you know what else?

What?

I liked it when you called me "Baby."

Then she settled back into bed, and Mo accepted her completely.

The cabin they had rented was some ways South of the lake, but it could still be heard. It was late in the season, and most of the rooms were empty and silent. The one they had rented was not unlike a tiny New York studio apartment, consisting of an oblong room with a kitchen and a bathroom partitioned off with temporary walls on one end, and a working stone fireplace and hearth on the other. The windows provided little in the way of a view, but they were on the top floor of the building, and there was a skylight in the ceiling facing to the North. When they finally both escaped from the bed, they got dressed and went out walking up Canada Street in search of a late lunch, hungry enough to stop at the first Bar and Grill they found.

It was a clean, well-lit sort of place, and the two of them sat at a table out on the deck lined with the late-day shadows of a nearby tree. In the offing lay the lake. The lunchtime crowd had dispersed, and dinner was still a couple of hours away, and only one other table was occupied. Two waiters were working the place, and even though they had nothing immediate to do, they waited a moment for Marty and Mo to settle into their seats before approaching with menus.

I'm Craig, and this is Kerry. Since we're not what you'd call "slammed" at the moment, you guys get both of us.

They each ordered a tall cold one, and when they had drank those down, they ordered another round along with their sandwiches. In the short time that it took them to wolf those down, the shadows had completely covered their table and the breeze had picked up enough to stir up a hissing sound among the leaves in the tree. They ordered another round of beers, pitted Rick Blaine against Charles Foster Kane in a boxing match, got the next round on the house ("Good luck," Craig said, rapping his knuckles twice on their table), talked about what they wanted out of life and whether it was too much to hope for or even hold onto were they to fulfill those needs, and ordered yet another round. Marty excused herself for the bathroom, and Mo took the opportunity to step outside and smoke half a cigarette. By the time they were finally ready to settle their tab, the meager dinner crowd had already come and gone. When they left, instead of heading back down Canada Street, they walked over to the water. The sun had already dipped below the horizon, but there was still enough light bouncing around in the atmosphere for them to be able to see the low rolling Adirondack foothills on the East shore of the lake. When they finally left the last streetlight behind them and reached the towpath along the edge of the water, Mo and Marty stopped and kissed in the bituminous dark. Back in the cabin, Mo watched as Marty removed her shirt, exposing the small muscles of her back and shoulders. Then he embraced her from behind, smelled her hair, and looked up through the skylight above, where he could see just about every star that existed in the diaphanous night.

In the morning, it was Mo's time to wake up early. The bedside note he left was identical to hers: *Went for a walk. Back soon. M.* After closing the door softly behind him, he headed off towards the Southern lip of the lake. When he reached the water's edge, he turned and began to follow it. A slight though welcome breeze was in the air and it lent just a bit of texture to the surface of the water. There were more hemlocks, beech, and sugar maple trees and far fewer Dutch elms, but in some ways Mo found himself reminded of the North Woods in Central Park. Whenever something was bothering him enough to keep him from sleeping, Mo would leave his apartment in the dawn and walk East down the block towards Strangers' Gate. He had always liked that particular entrance, for it seemed (at least to him) the sort of place where unknown, faceless individuals with little or no identity beyond hazy European names like Jean-Marc or Chantal would come together for inflamed, anonymous, amorous trysts consisting of as much unity as they did brevity. As he walked up the three steep flights of stairs, he would occasionally conjure up images of girls from his past, and have them walk with him. He reminded himself of the pleasures he had felt in each of their beds, and each morning after gave him the same sense of unconfinement that he got on these walks upon cresting the Great Hill and looking out across the lawn. After circling around to the other side of the Hill, Mo proceeded across West Drive, and stepped down into the North Woods. He and the woman of his memory followed the Loch that cut its way through the Ravine towards the great, hulking Huddle-stone Arch. There, like the water does, he would stop, perhaps paus-ing to recall his bar tab from the night before, or to reflect upon other, more ancient longings and regrets. The woman he most often carried with him was named Jackie, whom he had fallen for as that last leaf which falls from an autumn tree to complete a red-and-yellow drift into which they might have jumped, laughing, hand in hand, if only he had ever found it in himself to tell her that he loved her so. From the one night that they ever spent together, he remembered lying on his back in her bed and looking up at her as she straddled his legs with her own. Her sweater was off, and Mo reached up to take the gentle heft of her ample, teardrop breasts in his hands. She looked down and smiled at him, and he felt safe and happy and humble, as if she were the sun and he a lonesome dusty road running along beneath her. He remembered the soft curves of her strong legs, which he had gazed upon for hours long after she had fallen asleep, and he remembered thinking that it was the most tender thing he had ever seen in his life, resting there, exposed by a tug of the sheet. It seemed so tender, in fact, that he could not bring himself to touch it, and instead he held its image in his mind so tightly that now it had become more than a memory: it was a remedy against the slow and inexorable passage of time and the pain of broken things left in its wake. Still, though, it was merely a diminution of what was once a very real thing. *When will I see you again? That was the last thing she ever said to me. That's the kind of memory that grips you as if with talons. The kind that leaves an ineradicable scar on the spirit like the loss of romantic innocence or the taking of another man's life. The happy memories are the ones that you yourself have to try and cling to for the rest of your life. Until death do you part with your past. That's what I'll be thinking about when I die: that the last day of a waning life is the only one you will never be doomed to remember.* At this point, if he were in the North Woods, Mo would be rounding the bend at the Waterfall and crossing the little stone bridge over the stream; here at the Lake, he was standing on the slopes of French Mountain. There was still fog on the water, but on a clear morning, from that point, he could have looked North across thousands of acres of water, all the way to Shelving Rock and Tongue Mountain.

When he got back to the cabin, Marty was just getting out of the shower. She spoke while drying her hair with a towel.

We're meeting Kerry and Craig for dinner tonight.

Are we?

Yes, Kerry called this morning and invited us back to their restaurant. They're off tonight, so we're dining with them on the house!

I didn't even know they had your number.

When you stepped out to smoke last night, Kerry and I started talking. She's Canadian. She used to work in Quebec City for a small cruise line that runs back and forth along the St. Lawrence River, doesn't that sound amazing? To always be on the water like that? Always on the move? To just keep going and going and going, maybe even forever? Anyway, she met Craig on one of those trips, and moved down here to be with him.

Sounds good to me. What time are we meeting them?

They spent the afternoon lounging around the cabin, with Marty writing some ad copy for a new book and Mo thumbing his way through a copy of *Bodega Dreams*. They left just before nightfall and took the same towpath they had walked home along the night before. There was a narrow spit of muddy beach along the edge of the lake, and a great blue heron was standing there on spindly legs, scanning the shallows for small fish. When it became aware of them, its head snapped up, its long neck erect, and watched them for a fraction of a second before launching itself into the air with a series of graceful, powerful, arcing strokes of its wings. The last thing they could see as it beat on, low across the water, was its white scut flashing in the declining light. Marty was struck breathless.

That's what I was trying to tell you about! That's what I was looking for in the jewelry; that's what's supposed to be in love. In that bird! The strength and the grace of it!

They arrived at the restaurant soon thereafter. The four of them sat around a table for eight out on the deck, the empty seats occupied by alternating pitchers of iced tea and beer, a bottle of Patrón, and an assortment of shot and pint glasses. In the center of the table were plates of quesadillas, baskets of fries, and other standard bar fare appetizers. Blue methylene neon lights flashed and glared around the bar inside, but the natural light illuminating their table was as mild as the surface of the lake itself. Marty was controlling most of the banter, but after a few drinks, Mo opened up a bit himself.

So Kerry, Marty tells me you're from Quebec?

Yeah, I'm Québécois. For the most part, anyway.

But you don't even have an accent.

My dad's from Vermont.

Do you even speak French?

Il faut que vous parliez aussi.

Solo hablo español. Pois, eu falo um poquinho português.

Eu também. Grandparents in Nova Scotia.

Porra!

So, you wanna know what they call maple syrup in French?

What is this, *Pulp Fiction?*

Kerry smiled.

They call it "sirop."

They both laughed. Craig and Marty wouldn't have understood, but they weren't listening anyway, locked in their own mini conversation.

So do you have a Canadian passport?

Nope. I actually never had a passport.

So how do you get back and forth across the border?

Your government is ridiculous, that's how. There's a checkpoint on I-91, but if you get off at the last exit and take the side roads through the town of Derby Line, all of a sudden you see signs in French and distances in kilometers, and poof, you're in Rock Island, Quebec. People have been taking that route forever. Like, even back in the day, Ernest Hemingway used to go through there on his way from Windsor up North to his fishing grounds.

Sounds kind of like the way El Paso and Ciudad Juárez used to be. Grande on one side, Bravo on the other. You just pay up, and cross the Santa Fé Bridge. No document check. Nobody even looks at you.

Crazy, isn't it?

Yeah. It's nuts. After 9/11, everyone is all riled up about the Southern border, but nobody's worried about the big old Maple Menace. Canadians. They walk among us.

Kerry laughed again.

Canadian Bacon was a prescient movie, wasn't it?

Yes it was.

So were you in New York on 9/11?

Yeah.

Could you see anything?

Yeah. Everything.

What happened?

I was coming in from Brooklyn. Just got off the 4/5 train at 14th Street. And these people, hundreds of 'em, were just standing there, frozen, looking up into the sky. I even saw one guy just staring through a pair of binoculars. It was as if the whole island was on pause, except for the flames and the smoke. You know, it was kinda eerie, like I had just stumbled into some kind of Falun Gong meditation or something, like those terracotta warriors in China, guarding their emperor even after death. But then the South Tower buckled and went, and all those statuesque people started to book it. I didn't know what to do, so I headed towards my friend's apartment. He was working for Merrill at the time, but somehow he made it out of the financial district and back up to his rig safe enough. Not sound, but safe enough. All the cell phones were still jammed up, so we went to the Heartland Brewery on Union Square to have lunch. To have lunch, and to wait. Can't remember what I had. Roast beef sandwich, I think. Anyway, on that day, they were still open for lunch.

Kerry exhaled deeply. Mo took a mouthful of ice from one of the empty glasses. They had been downing drinks at quite a rate, and he was starting to feel the saliva gathering in his mouth that indicated his stomach was nearing full capacity.

Patrón is some smooth shit, but I know I'm in trouble because I've lost count.

So you're not gonna slurp the worm?

Tequila doesn't have a worm. You're thinking of mescal.

What's the difference?

It's like squares and rectangles, or dogs and puppies. Tequila is a kind of mescal, but mescal isn't necessarily a kind of tequila. It's more generic. Understand?

Nope.

Tequila is only made in Tequila, which is a region of the state of Jalisco. Mescal can be bottled anywhere.

How do you know all this? You're not even Mexican...

I'm a drinker. And you know what they say...

What?

That makes me a citizen of the world. If you ever need some advice on pisco or aguardiente, just give me a call.

Oh, so it's kind of like champagne and sparkling white wine in France.

Exactly. You know, that reminds me of a toast...

Kerry roused Craig and Marty from their own involved conversation. Glasses up!

Here's to champagne for my real friends, and real pain to my sham friends!

Glasses were clinked and drained. When Craig slammed his down on the table, he turned to Mo.

I'm gonna have a smoke. You want one?

Yeah, thanks man. I could use one.

They walked over to the opposite side of the deck, so as not to bother the ladies. There, Craig shook two American Spirits out of his pack and handed one to Mo. After lighting up, he took in a lungful of smoke and held it for a moment before releasing it out into the night air above his head.

Looks like you and Kerry are getting along.

Yeah, somehow we got started talking about Canada and tequila and shit.

Craig laughed.

If it was Canadian tequila, I'd be worried. But that's cool.

How long have you two been together?

Maybe two years now. Something like that. Listen...

Craig took another long drag. Before he exhaled, he looked directly at Mo. There was an intensity there, the kind that can send an unwanted message with more terseness than a telegram.

Listen, this is really the first time we've even spoken. We're basically strangers. And somehow, that makes it easier for me to just up and ask you this. So what is up with you and this girl?

Mo didn't even notice that he hadn't called Marty by name. His ultimate answer, though, would have been no different.

Why do you ask?

I guess Kerry and Marty were talking last night and this morning, and she kind of gave up her whole story. About the failed pregnancy, the failed engagement, and man to man I'm just wondering if you know what you're getting into.

Mo took a moment to gather up an answer inside of him before replying.

It'd be too easy to say that I'm in love with her or anything like that. But I'm happy now. It might be an emotional shitstorm for her right now, but at least I know which way the wind is blowing. For me, that's what makes this whole thing peaceful. Even moreso than this lake. *And how peaceful it must be come fall, come the first touch of cold, with the multicolored leaves wafting down over the surface of the water, falling towards their own reflection the way we fell in love with each other, and solitude ripples away across the lake.*

All I'm saying is this: make sure you're not just thinking about yourself. Think about her, too. You know, look both ways before you cross the street, and all that kind of shit.

That's exactly what I'm talking about. I believe in her. It might be a judgment call, but it's a judgment call that I'm willing to make. If I didn't believe in her, I never would have come up here.

I understand, but still, I can't help but wonder... if she believed in herself, she would have left him a long time ago.

Mo shot a hard look back at him, but kept his thoughts to himself. *It's because she's not a quitter. And she's not going to quit on me now. There's a part of her that he never reached, the part that allows us to love love. It's the truth. I don't have to sell myself on it. I don't have anything to be afraid of. Not the panic, the trembling, the anxieties, the unease that comes with the fear to love. No. This ardor comes not from hesitation but from faith.*

I'm not being blind about this, if that's what you think.

I'm just saying. But you don't want to be stubborn about it either. A wise man once said that stubbornness can be either your best friend or your worst enemy.

And I've got a concrete head and a re-bar mind, is that what you're saying?

Craig threw his butt on the ground, exhaled a plume of smoke, and crushed it with his boot. Then he offered a lighthearted chuckle.

Fuck it. Let's go back in. I'd rather hear another one of those toasts of yours, anyway.

Back inside, Marty and Kerry were laughing it up at the table. They tried to muffle themselves as the men returned to the table. Kerry spoke.

Welcome back to the party!

Listen, Big Mo's got another big toast for us.

Craig didn't even sit down; he just grabbed the nearest half-full glass and raised it.

Take it away, Mo.

Mo brought his own glass up on high. Kerry and Marty followed.

Salud, amor, y pesetas, y el tiempo para gustarlos.

Before even taking a drink, Kerry exclaimed,

I love it!

Actually, sometimes I think it sounds better in English. If you switch around "love" and "health" and then change "pesetas" to...

But she cut him off right there.

No! It's perfect just the way it is.

The two couples continued to eat, drink, and be merry until the porters arrived to clean the establishment. When Marty and Mo finally returned to their cabin it was more early than late. There was a surge of grey light on the lake, cut only by the long, slow, lupine howl of a loon. They fell asleep together, still fully clothed, still shivering in the morning cold and at each other's touch. When he woke, Mo went out behind the cabin and to gather some dry kindling and logs with which to build a fire. In a place like this, fall officially starts on Labor Day, not on the autumnal equinox, and that year the warm weather seemed to have left with the tourists and vacationers. When he went back inside, Marty was awake, and a pot of coffee was percolating in the kitchenette. It was still there at noon, when they woke up for the second time that day. Mo was lying on his back with Marty to his side, turned towards him, her leg slung across his, her head tucked in he hollow between his shoulder and neck, her breathing relaxed and soft and slow. They lay together wordlessly until the sound of a car passing by on the road finally roused them. Marty stretched and spoke, her eyes still closed.

I think I'll go for a swim.

What? You're insane. The water's gotta be in the fifties!

It's not that cold. Besides, I'm tough.

She smiled. Mo smiled too.

You are such an interesting person.

Marty eased her way out from under the sheets and sat up at the edge of the bed. He watched as she stood up, revealing her waist, her hips, her legs, and watched as her bare feet padded across the floor like those of a cat. Mo hadn't even thought to bring a bathing suit with him, as was a bit surprised when Marty opened one of her suitcase, pulled one out, stepped into it and tugged it on. She grabbed a beach towel on her way out, and the last thing he thought before the screen door slammed shut behind her was that her skin was still very white, and her freckles were still minutely visible.

Eventually Mo got up himself, poured a cup of coffee, and stepped out onto the tiny porch outside the cabin. Marty's fascination with swimming was something of an enigma to him. She only did it alone; even if she were going to a crowded public pool in the summer, she never invited a friend to go with her. *It's a solitude of her own design. A liquid solitude spent among the lapping waves.* Mo sat down in a lawn chair and reminisced about the cloudy day he spent on Staten Island's South Beach, in the shadows of the expansive Verrazano. He remembered standing on the pier and looking at the three layers of brown that were spread out before him: the wooden planks of the boardwalk, the cumin-colored sand, and the murky water beyond. Later he, like her, went for a swim. In fact, he spent the rest of the day in the surf, let the waves lift and drag and push and pull him back and forth, this way and that, and many hours later, as he lay down in his bed that night, it still felt as if his body was being swaying along with the waves. In a distant way, it reminded him of a concert he had been to in Central Park not long before; Victor Wooten was thumping away at a cover of the Beatles' "Come Together," and he could still feel the bass line pounding away in his guts later that same night. He sat there on his chair, reciting the wonderful, deliberate, irrational lyrics in his head, and realized that what he was experiencing there was a coincidence of togetherness. *She in the water, me with the music. Coming together unwittingly, attendant in thought, even across this physical distance. But soon she'll be walking back up this path. We will see each other, let our eyes do some of the talking for us. And I think they'll prove to be immune to solitude. I don't believe the language of loneliness can ever be translated through the eyes. And with what they say instead, we can have a lasting coincidence of togetherness, a synchronicity of waves, a deepening of the heart's rhythms, a true partnership of the eyes.*

Marty was gone for over an hour, but eventually she did come walking back up the path, her towel wrapped around her shoulders like a shawl. She was shivering and smiling to an equal degree, and tiny rivulets of water trickled through her sleek, black hair and cascaded down over her body. Mo hustled to collect some clean, dry towels and an oversized (for her) hooded sweatshirt with the words "Prairie Lights

Dog Patrol" emblazoned across the chest before going out to meet her.

Jesus, you look pretty fucking hot for a girl with hypothermia.

She laughed and brushed her lips across his as she shuffled past him and into the cabin.

While she warmed herself back up in the shower, Mo took up position in the kitchenette and got started on lunch. Two cans of tomato soup went into a pot along with a few shakes of garlic powder, and a few slices of provolone cheese were sandwiched between four thick slabs of rye bread spread with olive oil and dropped into a frying pan. When Marty, the soup, and the grilled cheese were all ready, they took their plates and went out onto the porch to eat.

When do you want to head back to the city? I don't have any meetings tomorrow so I can basically go in to the office any time. Do you have class or anything you need to get back for?

Fucking classes. Mo felt like he had just swallowed a lead sinker. He hadn't felt either needed or even welcome in class, never felt like he was a part of something bigger, something better, something that mattered. Going to class was something he quite literally dreaded, as if every hour he spent there was an hour he would later come to rue. When he had first begun his tour of such high education, it had felt in every way like a step towards a better life. Now he found himself mired in disgust. Instead of answering Marty's question, he looked out across the forested declivity of hills in the distance, surveying every ridge between the Northern and Southern points of the sun's annual swing. *And there are even more mountains behind this range, mountains and mountains, rolling low and away like waves retreating from a beach. It's a great big world out there, but somehow all I've been doing is rebreathing the same stale air over and over again. That's all this grad school stuff is, anyway. A flat fucking island in the middle of nowhere where swarms of migrating birds come to bark and quarrel with one another as they scrape out a tiny muddy space to call their own, even if they have to drive off one of their own kin to do it. So that's it. I refuse to fight for a spot to roost amongst the innumerable horde. I'll be the one that flies off to find the fresher air.*

Mo?

Sorry. I got distracted by a bird. Anyway, let's just get up early tomorrow morning. I'd like to spend one more night here at the lake. With you.

Marty smiled at him. They gathered their plates and went back into the cabin, closing the door behind them.

They left the lake the next morning at first light, and were back in the city before noon. Mo dropped Marty off at her Loisaida apartment, returned the car to the Enterprise location in Spanish Harlem, and began walking home, west along 110th Street. It was during that long, cross-town walk that something began happening to him, something indistinct which would nevertheless preoccupy him for months to come.

He spent his days at the bar. She spent her days at the office. They met for lunch, and slept in her bed. October came and went, and nights and mornings were becoming colder, but the days were completely unchanging. Long, quiet, indistinguishable days of monotony and routine. Leaves made the shift from colorful to dead, the snow fell and eventually melted, but the days themselves were invariable, sourceless, and directionless. With the threat of spring approaching, Mo realized that he was slowly, subtly, and silently going insane. He walked circles around his apartment, entering and reentering the empty rooms like a living ghost, and when that ceased to alleviate his depression, he walked circles around his familiar neighborhood. He smiled at all the usual faces, none of them ever knowing that he was now living in a giant sunlit prison of worry, sentenced to an undefined term. He worked off and on checking IDs at the Lion's Den, and in the meantime worried about things to come, about what would be next in store for Marty and him, and worse: *What if this is the change I have been waiting for? I have food, shelter, and the love of a woman, and yet I do nothing with it, I do nothing. I have no idea what I'm doing for myself, and I don't even notice the lost and irretrievable days on the calendar anymore.* From time to time during these anonymous, identical days, his attitude would swerve off this wistful path and into the oncoming traffic of anger. He felt stagnant, tired, and bored, as if Lilith herself had blinded him, seduced him, bound and gagged him. *The bitch. She sucked me into her own life and now she enjoys what I have sacrificed.* It was thus that Mo approached the summer, and—facing the impending anniversary of their earliest encounter—he decided to do something about what had happened.

Mo made dinner plans for Old Town on 18th Street, one of Marty's favorite after work spots. But he arrived in the middle of the afternoon; he hauled open the door, strode in beneath the shining, pressed-tin ceiling, and drew himself up to the long, lacquered bar. The place was sparsely populated, and a bartender was with him quickly.

What are you having today?

Shot of Jack and a Yuengling.

Need a menu or anything?

Nah boss. Can't afford the food, but I can't afford sobriety right now either.

He slapped two twenties down on the bar. The bartender took one, and a few minutes later, returned with his change and the two drinks. Mo emptied the shot glass in four or five sips, and downed the pint with an equal number of gulps. He stared at his reflection in the mirror behind the bar, wondering how he was going to do this. The bartender brought him another round, and again he drank the whiskey followed by the lager. Five o'clock came, and the after work crowd began to file in, eyes glazed over from staring at computer screens, fingers curled from hours of entering data into a keyboard, and tongues hanging loosely with an alcoholic thirst. They were the people who labored day after day under the flickering gloom of fluorescent lights only for the chance to emerge at dusk, to go out and replace those lights with the flickering gloom of neon bar ads without ever questioning their lives. And Mo drank, not with them but among them.

Marty entered later. Mo spotted her as soon as she opened the door and watched as she slid and sidled her way through the swarming mass of people at the bar. She was wearing a tailored yellow shirt, snug black slacks, and her bangs had fallen across one eye. She was carrying a jacket in one hand and a bag in the other, and Mo caught himself smiling as she tried to blow the tuft of hair away from her face. *She looks beautiful when she's exhausted. But her feet must be killing her.* Mo grabbed his change off the bar, hopped off his stool, and worked his way through the horde to meet her.

When did you get here?

I don't know. Let's go upstairs and see if there's a table.

By chance, there was a tiny table available there, nestled in next to the kitchen. Mo sat down quickly and heavily, while Marty made no attempt whatsoever to disguise her weariness as she folded herself into the smallish chair. Her face was pale, her lips heavy, her eyes joyless and blunt.

Am I late? I'm sorry, I was stuck on a conference call...

Don't worry about it. Are you hungry? Let's get someone over here...

They ordered their usual burgers and drank their usual beers. Marty was indeed hungry; she ate quickly and silently through most of dinner, leaving Mo to wonder how he was going to broach the subject.

Eventually, though, Marty paused for a moment, took a sip of beer, and leaned back against the seat. She sighed.

God, I have to go to this damn conference this weekend.

Where is it?

Upstate aways. At a big resort hotel near New Paltz. I really don't want to go.

Really?

Mo said this softly, almost meekly, before continuing with a more optimistic tone.

You'll probably like it better once you're up there, though. You'll be back up in the mountains, like at Lake George. They've got a spa there, right? You could get a treatment, you could go swimming, you could do whatever.

Marty froze in her seat. Her hands tensed up, and she held her breath for a long moment before whispering a reply.

I'll like it better? I'll be back in the mountains? I'll get a spa treatment? Mo, what are you talking about?

I don't know. Look, it just seems like we've been going in circles a lot lately. Like we're going through the motions.

Marty looked aghast.

Mo...

Baby I'm just looking for a way to change things up. To make something new, to do something new for myself...

Oh no... Jesus God, no, no...

Her once blunt eyes were suddenly alive with panic. She lurched across the table, knocking over a beer and grabbing Mo's forearm with both hands.

It's for us... I'm doing all of this for us... so we can be even more together than we already are...

Baby what are you talking about?

Oh God, I'm so sorry, I just didn't know...

Didn't know what?

That you felt this way...

Her panicked eyes were filling with tears now. *It was as if our life together had been as smooth and yet as tenuous as the surface of a pond on a calm day, and the slightest breeze broke the surface tension and set the waters in motion.*

Marty what do you mean, you're doing all of this so we can be more together?

I'm so sorry, I should have known...

Mo put his free hand on top of hers, which were still gripping his forearm.

Baby, just tell me?

She exhaled deeply before continuing.

I'm not going to a conference, okay?

What are you talking about?

I'm going up to look for a house...

A house?

I should have told you... I mean, I was just so wrapped up in the idea. Maybe that's why I didn't notice how you were feeling. How things were changing, or not changing, or whatever. I just wanted it to be a surprise. A gift.

It's okay, just relax. You can tell me now. Just take it easy.

I've been up there a couple of times before. For interviews. They want me to be their new marketing manager.

At the resort?

Yes. Yes.

Marty, that's amazing...

This isn't how I wanted to do it. Not like this.

So what? Who cares? You can do it now. You can tell me now just the way you planned it...

I don't know. You were right though. It reminded me of the time we spent at Lake George. I guess I wanted to try and recreate that. But not the vacation part. I wanted to make it permanent, like the jewelry. You know, buy a house. So we could be together. Live together. Sleep together every every night. I just wanted a place that would hold us together...

She's right. This is what it's always been for, the patience to wait for change to come, the persistence it took to live on the cusp between one day and the next for so long, the reason for enduring the unwavering, monotonous solitude of the repeated days. It's all becoming true, and who cares how or why.

Marty, that's the most beautiful thought I've ever heard.

Really?

Yes. And you're right. It's not just going to be you. It'll be us. We will like it better. Together. We will be back in the mountains. Not just you. We.

You mean you'll think about it?

I mean I'll do it. For us.

It was as if the entire restaurant outside their tiny booth vanished, leaving only them. Marty sounded almost chipper when she spoke.

Jesus I was so scared, I had no idea how I was going to bring it up to you. I was afraid you'd say no.

Well look at me! I was all worked up because I wanted this to happen. I mean, I was starting to get scared that it never would.

At least now we know that we are safe enough to be scared. As long as it's with each other. Together.

Yes, yes.

They say there can be no courage without fear, and I'll add to that the suggestion that courage has less to do with real, God-fearing faith than it does with a belief in good, old fashioned, pure dumb luck. I just didn't believe it at the time. It was overshadowed by time, actually; by the length of time we had already spent together without so much as a hint of either miracle or disaster. It's like electricity: the current of time just runs through you, but you can only take it for so long before you have to let go of the wire and find out which side of the gorge you land on.

They kissed each other from across the table, and spent the rest of dinner imagining the pedestrian routines of their upcoming life together with a very naïve excitement. They walked down the stairs hand in hand, but Marty held up just before they reached the door to the street.

Thank you for this gift.

Mo looked into her eyes, which had gone from blunt to panicked to tearful to joyful in the past two hours alone.

Marty, you are a gift. Always remember that.

She smiled, feeling a fullness, a sense of wholeness. They stepped out into an unusually warm evening though perhaps it just felt like one, their faces flushed with fervor as they strolled down the sidewalk, the ephemeral taxis, like time itself, flying past them down the avenue, to the point where everything—themselves included—merged seamlessly into the oncoming night.◆

The Lantern

THE FIRST THING WILLIE DID when he woke up the next Sunday was take a shower. It had been an unusually hectic night at the diner, and his skin and hair were still imbued with the heavy smells of bacon fat and pepper sauce. He stood there under the showerhead for an extended length of time, and when the bathroom had been completely filled with steam, he shut off the water and stepped out onto the damp floor. Then he shaved off the previous week's growth, pausing every thirty seconds or so to re-clear the misty mirror. Finally, he toweled himself off, walked around the corner to his bedroom, and put on a clean pair of boxers and a clean shirt. *Fuck. A three-day-old pair of jeans will have to do, I guess.* He was brewing a pot of coffee from grounds he'd helped himself to from the dry storage room when there was a knock at the door. It was Al.

After a cup's worth of coffee each, they walked over to the Dean for brunch. In the light of day, Willie picked up a few more details about this skinny, short-haired thirty-something girl which he hadn't noticed during their previous encounter. Her skin was darker than his, but he wasn't sure if it was just tanned. And her hair wasn't just Dutch Boy or Pixie-style short; it was Marine-style short. Like it had been haphazardly hacked off with a set of electric clippers, and then, as it was growing back, had been given some semblance of style with gel and a Kool-Aid dye job. Willie wondered silently whether she was gay. He guessed (or perhaps he hoped) that she wasn't. She had a flat backside, but her chest was clearly artificially inflated. Stripper boobs, he thought, though the rest of her body was wafishly thin. The further they walked, the more intrigued Willie was by this very new, very inimitable friend.

When they got to the Dean, they sat in the back patio, ordered Bloody Marys with their prix-fixe brunch, and gazed upon the current exhibit by a local Brooklyn artist that was being displayed there at the tavern: A Photographic Study of the Urban Farms of East New York. Al was the first to comment.

Farms? They call those farms? That's barely a garden!

Hey, what do you know about farms, anyway? You're from Queens! Don't tell me you're giving in to that whole Brooklyn envy thing...

Well, since you asked, I know because my cousin owns a huge greenhouse in Colombia, on the Sabaña de Bogotá.

So, what does he do? Grow coca leaves?

I knew you were gonna say that. But no, damn it! He grows flowers, okay? The best fucking flowers on earth, as a matter of fact. Roses, orchids, chrysanthemums of any color you want. Even alstroemerias. Do you know what those are?

Do I look like a botanist to you?

Al laughed.

I was just testing to see if you spoke Spanish. It's a kind of lily.

¿Como un lirio? ¿Un liro de los valles?

This time, Al shrieked with joy.

I knew it! Anyway, it's a huge industry.

Really? I had no idea.

That's because the only time you hear anything about Colombia in the news, it's drug trafficking or kidnapping or corrupt politicians and stuff.

Actually, that last one happens here a lot, too.

Anyway, yeah, it's big business. There's even a National Association of Flower Exporters.

That's kind of cool, actually.

Yeah, man. Fair trade ain't just for coffee anymore!

They both laughed.

So yeah, that's how I know a farm when I see one.

Okay, okay, I'll concede the point.

Now it's your turn. Tell me something about yourself that I wouldn't have expected.

Willie paused, draining the last of his Bloody Mary, and looked at the table in front of him. So far, he'd eaten a biscuit and most of the fresh fruit, and was nearing the end of his corned beef hash with poached eggs. Al had finished her drink as well, and he motioned to the waiter for another round. But even after buying all of this time, he still wasn't sure how he would respond. This was the second time in a week—actually, the second time at this very establishment—that someone had asked about his background. *With Kenyatta, Dante, and Equality, it was easier. It sounded like they might have had some experience of their own with that sort of thing. Plus, with them, I wasn't trying to... but what am I trying to do with this girl, Al, anyway? Get to know her? Jesus, that sounds so fucking trite. I could just lie. Just make some shit up. Like that guy I used to know who told every girl he ever met that his name was Jay. His real name was Corey, but they never knew that, and they didn't know that he wasn't really from Teaneck, but rather from the projects off the J train in Brooklyn.*

Um, let's see. Well, I grew up with Pedro Martínez.

Am I supposed to know who that is?

Willie grinned. Inside, he breathed a sigh of relief. *It doesn't even matter whether that's true. Just keep the subject away from how I ended up here.*

So lemme tell ya, I know I work at the diner up on Washington and all, but I gotta admit, this place is absolutely phenomenal.

You know what? That's the second time you've used that word around me.

What word?

Phenomenal. And you said it the same way both times. Fuh-NAW-min-uhl.

Aren't you the observant one?

Actually, it's me who's been doing the observing. Like how she's got a picture of Joshua Redman on her T-shirt, and how his face is all distorted across her chest. And how, ever since we've sat down, she's eaten a whole half a biscuit, and without any butter or jam either. What is with this girl? She drinks like a fish, but she's barely touched her food. I wonder if she's anorexic or something like that...

The early brunch crowd was starting to disperse, and orders for eggs and toast were being replaced by chicken parm sandwiches and buffalo burgers. Overhead, the sun had passed its zenith and was beginning its long, lethargic descent across the sky. Shadows slowly ran to hide underneath the patio tables. When the waiter next came to their table on his rounds, Al petitioned for a round of beers instead of a third Bloody Mary.

On Sundays, I can only serve you splits until 4 o'clock. House rules. Would you still like a couple?

Only splits? Are you sure?

Yes, ma'am.

Is Mick here yet?

Yes, ma'am he is.

Tell him that his real estate girl is here, and ask him if it's okay for her to order a couple of pints.

Sure thing. I'll be right back.

Willie was rather impressed, and it showed on his face when he spoke.

Wow. So that's what you do here, huh? How long have you been doing that?

I dunno, I got my license maybe a year or two ago? It wasn't exactly my first career choice. Anyway, I ended up at a little brokerage firm down near Atlantic. And when the owner here wanted to open a new restaurant, I ended up doing the deal for this place. Crown Heights is kind of my zone of sale, you know?

Gotcha.

So what were you doing before you changed up and applied for your license?

Al avoided answering just long enough for their pints to arrive. Only it wasn't the waiter who brought them out. It was a good-looking, long-haired, amiable man who spoke with what Willie thought was the slightest hint of a British accent. Al stood up to hug him before he even had a chance to set the beers down on the table.

Mick Pearce! How are you?

I'm fine, he finally said after setting down the glasses. But what about yourself? How's the treatment going? Have you had any more MRIs?

Al looked slightly uncomfortable, slightly sheepish at these questions. Willie got the acute and distinct impression that he wasn't supposed to know that she was sick.

I'm doing good. Real good. But more importantly, Mick, this is Willie. He's kind of new to the neighborhood.

Willie stood up; they shook hands.

Good to meet you. And good to know that Alba here is bringing in new business!

Actually, I was in here a few nights ago. I met… what's his name… the bartender…

Oh yeah, you met Dave. He told me that there was a new fish in the pond. Anyway, welcome to the tavern. You two enjoy.

As Mick returned to the duties of ownership, Al downed half of her beer in a single slug. When she came up for air, she looked uninclined to speak, so Willie pressed her with a question.

Sounds like you've been dealing with some tough shit.

Yeah. You could say that.

You want to talk about it?

Al didn't, not for another couple of beers, anyway. But when she did, the story that she told Willie was one of the most lamentable, almost dirge-like things he had ever heard. She talked about how, four years earlier, she was happily married, looking at buying a home just north of the city, in Nyack. They even had a property picked out: a spacious acre-and-a-half lot, with a custom built house only twenty years old, with a first floor master bedroom and attached office that they were planning on turning into a nursery in the very near future. But sadly, shockingly, while taking a shower one morning less than a week before closing on the deal, she found a lump in her left breast. She talked about scheduling her first MRI, and about what it was like when the results from that were still inconclusive. She talked about having a tissue biopsy done, and about getting the phone call from her doctor, who said that it came back positive. She talked about how she sank down right there, on the kitchen floor, crying and shaking for hours without ever even hanging up the phone. And she admitted that it was awkward—almost embarrassing, she said—for her to talk with her male oncologist in such clinical, technical, even sterile ways about a part of her body that was so often regarded as simply a plaything. She talked about how, for a time, her world became a whirlwind of decisions. Chemo or radiation. Mastectomy or lumpectomy. Have the genetic test or not. And she talked about how, in the midst of all those questions, she was able to come to the realization that, despite the fact she was only starting out on the path to treatment and recovery, she already knew that she never, ever wanted to walk down it a second time. That was when she decided to undergo a double mastectomy. She talked about how the chemo and hormone therapies left her too nauseous to eat and too exhausted to reach the bathroom if she ever did have to vomit. She talked about what it was like to watch yourself slowly, inevitably becoming a thirty-something woman without hair, without periods, and without breasts. She talked about what it was like to live as such, about what it was like to live with chest expanders that look so garish and monstrous that people often assumed silently that she was a stripper. And she talked about what it was like to live with a husband who hadn't touched her in months. About how they began to fight more and more, to a point where it was almost a daily occurrence. And about her decision to divorce him after he once grew so angry at her for her condition that he called her "selfish." She talked about finding a support group for cancer survivors, about forging friendships and learning from other women who had endured similar, devastating events. And she talked about how the horrible, God-awful truth of the matter was that some of those friendships she'd been forming were with people who were slowly, inevitably dying.

Willie's eyes were wide throughout this story, but it was Al's final words that struck him the most.

I'm thirty-five years old, and I've gone to three weddings. But I had to stop counting the number of funerals I've gone to after one year with cancer.

Willie was silent, almost paralyzed, until she spoke again.

Anyway, that's what Mick was talking about.

It must have been terrifying.

You know, it's strange. But for me, the diagnosis wasn't the scary part. I was more afraid about what it was costing me in terms of my identity, about what it was taking away from me. You know, my husband, my home, my life, everything. I don't mean literally taking my life... I mean, taking away life as I knew it. The life I had come to know and understand.

Things aren't supposed to change like that.

No they are not.

So how do you feel now? I mean, not just physically, but about all the changes?

You know, sitting here in this place, on a sunny afternoon, talking to you... I have to admit, I feel pretty good. But there was a time when I felt like life was doing whatever it wanted with me. I felt like a rowboat in the middle of the ocean during a hurricane.

How long did that last?

My grandparents in Colombia had a saying. It was something like, "a burro will work for you for ten years just for one chance at kicking you in the stomach." Well, I got kicked. Real fucking hard. And I don't know how long it felt like that. But I learned one thing: after awhile, if you can hold on long enough, it doesn't feel like pain or fear or anything like that anymore. Maybe it's just the eye of the hurricane, but at least you're not caught in the middle of a storm anymore. You're just out there, on the ocean. And maybe there's no land in sight, no boundaries or borders or anything, but at least the water is calm. At least…it is for a time.

You know, this probably isn't even comparable, but when I was a young kid, I was diagnosed with tuberculosis. I mean, I was infected, but I wasn't coughing up blood or anything. Anyway, I had to take antibiotics every day for nine months to kill the bacteria in my lungs before they became active. That's when one of my mother's friends told me she thought God was trying to send me a message.

Fuck, what was that even supposed to mean? What kind of message does God send via tuberculosis?

I don't know. I was really confused. I mean, we weren't even a very religious family. But this woman, she was a devout Pentecostal to the point of being just plain crazy. At least, that's what I thought. But it pissed me off, though. It pissed me off because it scared me. And it scared me because I wasn't a man of faith.

Are you now?

No. I've just never felt the need for there to be an entity like God in my life. I don't need the idea of God to explain the world, or how I'm supposed to live and die in it. And I decided that—even when I was sick—I didn't need that entity then, either. I guess I was a skeptic right from the start. I figured this woman was trying to pull some trick on me. Suggesting I had to make some arrangement with the old guy with a beard who lives up in the clouds. I don't make deals or compromise myself for fogs and mist. I'm not for some sort of entity, but I'm not against one either. I just am. I'm just me. And everything I say comes from my mouth and my mouth alone.

He looked to Al for affirmation, though what he saw in her eyes was something closer to recognition. But what she felt in her heart and what she told Willie were two different though not mutually exclusive things:

I think my faith is a complete and total understanding that my own cells have an inherent ability to become vicious little traitors. I never doubted the fact that I depended on them for life, but now I see—with neither fear nor astonishment—that they can have sudden, unexpected convictions of their own, and they will do whatever their DNA intends them to do.

You know what I believe in? I believe in my damn doctors. If you don't believe in them, it really doesn't matter what else you believe in. A person can't believe in his country if he doesn't believe in the army that's defending it.

You sound like a poet. Have you written any verses of your own?

Some.

I'd like to read something sometime.

Maybe.

Just then, a pained look came across her face, and she rubbed her shoulders one at a time, first the right and then the left.

Are you okay?

Al let a slight groan escape her throat.

I'm fine. It's just, after the surgery and treatment and everything, I have a lot of scar tissue. A lot of pain across my chest and shoulders.

So did they give you a bunch of meds or something?

They gave me so many damn pills. And half of them all start with "L." Letrozole, Lexapro, Lortab, Librium... it's just ridiculous. But I've got 'em all beat. I've got something better than any of them.

What's that?

BMT. Bob Marley Therapy.

Ah. I see. But didn't Bob die from cancer?

I didn't skip my chemo and prescriptions. But when it came to nausea and vomiting, a joint was the best thing I ever found. I couldn't eat without it. I'd be an anorexic cancer patient. As you can see, I haven't exactly stuffed my face full of food here.

She gestured at the leftovers still occupying their table.

And the pain?

It just relaxes me. Relaxes everything. Joints, muscles, scar tissue, everything. Speaking of which, I really need to step outside for a moment. Care to join me? I've got a one-hitter in my purse...

I'm afraid I can't partake, but I would most definitely love to join you.

They stepped out onto the sidewalk. The afternoon was rapidly morphing into dusk, and the neon beer signs in the windows had been turned on. It was what photographers and filmmakers call the magic hour, when the sun has just dipped beneath the horizon, leaving a soft, warm, almost liquid light to occupy the atmosphere for a few fleeting minutes. A crescent moon was already up; it hung there, slack in the sky, like a body slung in a celestial hammock. Al unzipped her purse and produced a small wooden case roughly the size of a deck of playing cards. She opened the top, pulled out the fake ceramic cigarette, and ground the end of it into the receptacle containing the marijuana. Then she stuck it between her lips, sparked her lighter, and inhaled deeply.

That feels so much better.

Al stood there, looking out into the dissolving light like an owl in the minutes before it goes out for its nightly hunt. Then she took the final hit from her pipe and spoke:

> She stood there on the sidewalk
>> In the duality of the evening
>>> Sun setting behind her
> And a moon three days from full
>> Rising high ahead.
>>> The sky was a martin's purple
> And flecked with traces of the cancer:
>> Threads of light like shooting stars
>>> In the brain more than the mind.
> Not knowing what else to do
>> She tried the futile exercise
>>> Of cataloging the forgotten names
> Of blues musicians, cuts of beef,
>> And Brooklyn neighborhoods.
>>> But she still knew what love was;
> That it was not unlike health,
>> In certain ways, and perhaps
>>> Even a misunderstood form of it.
> They had both traveled many miles
>> Along each of those two paths,
>>> And when they traveled separately
> They told the other of their journeys—
>> How they started out, and how they had arrived—
>>> So that the other might find
> Their own trail somewhat less thorny.
>> And yet they were still amazed
>>> At just how much they did not know

About the nature of the going itself,
    And about how many thorns still remained.
      What could be done,
Save for to hike on up the mountain
    And keep their eyes on the trees
      Instead of the thorns
Because once there was more blue
    Than green beyond the canopy,
      The two trails would converge, and
The summit would be at hand.

Willie stood there for a moment before speaking.

Let me guess... William Carlos Williams, right?

Al grinned widely.

What makes you think that?

He was a doctor. It sounded like something that might be from "Spring and All." You know, "By the road to the contagious hospital" and all that stuff.

Al's smile vanished softly as she answered.

I wrote that myself, shortly after my diagnosis. When my grandfather died, one of the things I kept was his old portable Underwood typewriter. And I still have it. I mean, I still use it. It's what I wrote that poem on.

Al took a deep sigh and stowed her equipment back in her purse before continuing to reminisce:

He had a tiny little plantation house in a village. It was on the Río de la Vieja, just a couple hours outside of Cali, which made it easy to ship the flowers he grew. The house was too small to have what you'd call an office or a study, so he put a chair and desk out on the back patio set up his typewriter and a tin of pipe tobacco, and banged out all his flower business documents right there. When the company became more successful, he had the patio enclosed in floor-to-ceiling windows, making it into a tiny greenhouse itself, so he could work among the flowers and look out over the brown, sandy river and the lush, verdant Santa Marta Mountains. I loved visiting him and that sunny little room. So when he died, I took the typewriter back to Jackson Heights with me, and now it's here in Brooklyn. I set it up on a little desk in front of a window, even though all it looks out over is the damp concrete courtyard in our building. And instead of the pipe tobacco, I keep my bowl there with a little dime bag of sin semilla.

It sounds like a magical memory of a magical place.

Oh, it's a very real one, believe me. Anyway, you wanna go back inside? I could use another drink...

They spent another couple of ours there at the tavern, drinking and debating everything from disease to poetry and music, eventually finding a coincidence of rhyme and light in Dylan Thomas and Common, to which they toasted:

"Dawn breaks behind the eyes, but it don't take a whole day to recognize sunshine!"

Willie did not have a shift at the diner that night, and they decided to settle up at the Dean and continue their association at Utopia. It was altogether dark when they stepped back out onto the sidewalk, the dissolving light now in full suspension, though by some retrograde effect their eyesight had sharpened, attuned to the midnight glow of an insomniac city. Willie realized that darkness can have its advantages, for it is not really a quality of light at all, but rather an opportunity to accept the other, more underappreciated senses. Perhaps even a sixth sense. *For I am aware of her there, walking along next to me, though we are not speaking, touching, or seeing one other. There is a gravity there, like a planet spinning through space, an atmosphere I can intuit, one that parts as she moves through it.*

Al walked quickly, the way New Yorkers will do whether they are running late for something or not. Willie was reminded of the old metaphor: are you walking the dog, or is the dog walking you? But at that moment, he really didn't care at all. He was actually quite happy not being in the lead, not being in control of things. He didn't even know how far he could trust this new woman who had so randomly appeared, rocking and rolling, into his life. She came across as unpredictable, though thoughtful and reflective at the same time. Willie decided he didn't know what to expect, and that he didn't really care anyway. He was ready for the unexpected. It made him feel liberated. It made him feel free.

There was a line outside the club, though no velvet ropes. After they positioned themselves at the end of it, Al spoke up.

Listen, I wanted to say thanks for listening to my sob story earlier. I promise I won't get all weepy on you. I've just gone through a lot of shit. I guess my life didn't quite turn out the way I thought it would, you know?

Willie knew. Willie knew only too well.

Hey, listen. Nobody ever knows what they're gonna get out of life. You're not alone in that.

It was a decent offering of support. At least, that's what he thought, until Al amended his statement.

But you are. I can see it. I can tell.

Willie looked back at her, surprised. Before he could come up with any sort of response, they were at the front of the line, facing the bouncer. Al was ushered inside, but Willie had to stop and get patted down before entering. The club itself looked much larger on the inside as it did on the outside. From the street, it was just a nondescript two-story brick building sitting on the point of a triangular corner with a poorly-lit blue and gold sign that read UTOPIA above the door. But once inside, the place revealed itself to be more like Mecca than Paradise, for it was thronged with what seemed like a full borough's worth of par-tygoers. It was old school night; the DJ in the booth was spinning Black Moon, Jeru the Damaja, and the obligatory Biggie Smalls. Most of the square footage was taken up by a dance floor, but the entire left side of the club was devoted to a long, shimmering bar. It was there that Al and Willie headed. After negotiating the crowd and getting an elbow on the bar, they ordered their respective drinks: a double Absolut cranberry and a Dos Equis. They stood there, side by side, drinks in hand, silently nodding their heads in time with the music. Slick Rick led to EPMD, which gave way to Rakim, but the dancers stopped grooving and threw up their hands when the opening strains of the Beatnuts' "Watch Out Now" boomed out of the venue speakers. Al cheered along with the rest of the crowd.

I love these guys! Psycho Les is Colombiano. He's from Jackson Heights, just like me!

And JuJu es un broder dominicano! I can't believe this qualifies as old school rap now. I never felt so old...

Hey, in hip hop, if you can last for ten years, you're a veteran!

They were just getting into the hook when the needle skipped off the record with an abrupt, amplified grating sound. As the speakers went silent, so did the crowd. Al and Willie strained to see what was going on; suddenly, the crowd started backing away from the DJ booth, where two large men stood nose to nose, jawing and posturing. Their voices could be heard clearly over the hushed floor.

I'll wet yo mark ass, bitch!

Fuck you, you maternity T-shirt wearing motherfucker!

The bouncers were just rushing in from outside when one of the two men suddenly drew a gun from his waistband. From that moment on, everything—even the chaos—seemed to happen in stark, exquisite relief. Willie could clearly see the thick, blunt barrel rise up vertical, the strobe-like muzzle flashes, and the simultaneous thuck-thuck-thuck of the report. Bits of the soundproof insulation that hung like stalactites from the ceiling of the cavernous room began to drift down slow as snow. And then the hysteria ensued. The air in the club took on the smell of firecrackers. Frantic screams curdled in throats. People scattered, scrambling, stumbling, tumbling to the floor, clambering to their feet, then lunging and plunging towards the exits. Al and Willie broke with them, pushed through the bottleneck at the door, and spilled out into the street. They paused, sucking in breath, before tearing off again, down the middle of the empty street. They could still hear the shouting behind them when another shot rang out, followed shortly by two more. Finally, they arrived back at their building, Willie panting, Al sobbing, both fumbling with their keys, terrified down to the very last second until they were finally inside and the heavy, reinforced door slammed home behind them. It was there, in the vacant hallway that they kissed. Hands grasped at each other's clothing, drawing their bodies together, ardent and fervent and made all the more so by the piquant mix of longing and fear. Somehow they found their way into Al's apartment, and from there on into the bedroom. Al collapsed onto her bed. There was a lava lamp on the nightstand which cast the entire room in a ghostly green light. Without sitting up, she began pulling off her shoes and socks.

I drink so fucking much. Can you get me a glass of water?

Willie smiled.

I think you drank just the right amount. But okay. Sure.

He went into the kitchen and opened the refrigerator door. It was still devoid of food. The Brita pitcher was there half full of water, but the leftover Bud from the party was gone. Willie grabbed the pitcher, found a glass in the cupboard, and filled it. When he returned to the bedroom, he saw that Al had finished stripping off the rest of her clothing.

Thank God.

Al took a sip and fell backwards onto her bed and closed her eyes.

Sometimes, all I want to do in the whole entire world is just surrender. Fuck it all, and surrender.

That was the last thing she said before passing out. Her respiration became slow and regular, and her chest rose and fell with each gentle breath. It was only then that Willie noticed the broad, transverse scars spanning her distended breasts. He hesitated for a moment, but then reached down and felt one. The scar itself was surprisingly smooth, and the tissue beneath it felt surprisingly dense, like the flesh of an apple. Then he shifted his eyes downward to examine the curly, exuberant hairs covering her feminine mound. Her body shivered softly, and Willie withdrew his hand. He wanted to touch her again, wanted to touch more of her, to discover more of this woman lying naked in front of him... But he did not. He simply inhaled the latent, mingling fragrances, and immediately he felt the effects of the alcohol vanish from his system. He was surprised by how aroused he was, gazing upon this scarred, frail body ravaged first by disease and then by treatment. *It must mean something. There must be something there. There has to be.* He watched her sleeping there for another minute, bathed in the lamp's greenish light, before covering her up with the sheet. Then he returned to his own apartment. Once again, it was late at night, the end of a long, fascinating, exhausting day, and yet Willie was nowhere near sleep even though the rolling, clattering shuttle train would soon be awake and moving. He sat down on his couch and closed his eyes, trying to imagine himself sitting in her grandfather's study back in Colombia and looking out across the mountains and the river valley. When he opened his eyes again, he got up and went over to his bookshelf where he selected a José Martí collection and a pen. When he found the poem he wanted, he wrote the following verses in the margin next to it:

Dos voces tiene ella: suya y el crepúsculo
Aunque muchas noches se confunden
Y cantan al unísono, unánime. Cierran
Mis ojos y ella me aparece como una tierra

No descubierta, desconocida, cogida
Entre la caída de la tarde y el nacer de la luna.
En noches como esta nos quedamos tan lejos,
Separados: el viento que canta en los cielos

Del firmamento estrellado y hermoso.
Pero sus voces, las dos, siguen llamando,
Y estoy en barco de vela, de viento,

Viniendo por su cuerpo ligero, inquieto,
Ni como el conquistador indigno, sino
Con el espíritu exploratorio del *voyageur*. ◆

The Valley

MO'S APARTMENT WAS SO MEAGERLY FURNISHED that it looked as if he was in a constant state of moving out. And after packing up enough clothes and things for an extended (daresay it, permanent?) stay with Marty, it looked no different at all. It would still be in his name for the time being—the University leased rooms in the building to students by the semester rather than the month—but that was merely technical. He looked around for his footprint, some bit of evidence that he had ever loved or even lived amid these walls, and all he saw were the cigarette scars on the squarish table in the kitchen, the sunken, onion-colored couch he often slept on, and the bookcase whose shelves were filled with books stacked flat instead of vertical. *And the gun. What the fuck am I going to do with that? There's no way I can take it to Marty's place... she'd kill me if she found it there, and King would kill me if he didn't find it here. Shit.* Mo looked around the large and largely empty room as if for help. Eventually, his eyes came to rest on the two S-hooks screwed into the ceiling where some former tenant had once hung a bicycle from its wheels, and Mo got an idea. Standing on one of the kitchen chairs, he was able to reach up and unscrew one of the hooks. Then he took both the hook and chair to the closet near the front door. Mo parted the hanging coats and jackets, set the chair inside the closet, and then wedged himself into the tight, available space and up onto the chair. He twisted around to face the closet door, and there, a foot or so above the horizontal door jamb, he screwed the hook back into the wall. After he tightened it as well as he could with his fingers, he hung the handgun from it by its trigger guard.

And that was it. Mo grabbed his two bags—one with his clothes, the other with his laptop—stepped out onto the landing, and punched the elevator button. When he exited on the ground floor, he paused for a moment, suddenly overtaken by the deep and unsettling notion that for some reason he may never see this foyer again. He dropped his bags and checked to make sure his keys were in his pocket, as if to prove that the place was still his, if indeed it ever had been. *So you can come back. You can always come back. It might not be much to look at, but there's something to be said for the security of always having a halfway decent old place to turn to. Using the old 'hood like collateral. Like a contingency plan.* Bolstered, he picked up his bags, leaned on the heavy outer door, and stepped out onto the street to hail a cab.

That night, he and Marty went out to their regular sawdusty dive bar to celebrate. Marty had agreed to take the marketing job at the big upstate hotel, but she wouldn't have to start until the following holiday season, when the resort would be initiating its new promotional strategy. They sat down at the same table as they had on so many other afternoons, surrounded by the same regular drinkers, the same table staff and bartenders, the same racks of spotted glasses, the same names and faces whom they now knew more as minor friends in the way that children will make friends at school whom they don't socialize with after class is dismissed. The waiter brought them their same beers, asked the same old questions about how they'd been, and then went back into the same closed kitchen.

Mo raised his glass.

To our new life together.

No. This one is to freedom.

Freedom?

From the lives we were living.

The glasses clinked together with a tone that rang as true, as perfect, and as pure as if they were struck by a tuning fork. There was something in the very pitch itself that made them feel harmonious and even happy enough to order dessert for a change: two glasses of port and a slice of cheesecake. They savored the sweet, fruity flavors in silence, and Mo found himself wondering indistinctly about what sorts of flavors a man dying of thirst might find in a glass of water. He was still somewhat absent in mind when Marty tipped back the dregs of her glass and said,

There are some people I want you to meet tomorrow.

Some people? Who's that?

Kim. I told you about her. She's the one who works in editorial upstairs from me. And her fiancé Elroy. He teaches English over at Stella Maris High School. I think you'll like them.

Mo nodded, feeling suddenly and newly presentable, and a few mornings later found him and Marty sitting on the same side of a booth at a midtown diner, waiting for the heretofore unacquainted friends to arrive. It was an unseasonably cold morning, and when the couple walked in, their faces were red and twisted in the way that people do when they are walking into a scalding headwind. Kim was clearly pregnant; Mo could see that before she even unbuttoned her coat. But when she tugged off her gloves to shake hands, he noticed no ring on her finger.

It's so good to finally meet you! Marty talks so much about you! And this is Elroy, she said with a nod.

Mo shook hands with both of them.

How you doing? Great to meet you too.

Sit down and warm up! Can you believe how late spring is this year? I mean, there's still all that disgusting black snow piled up on the curbs, Marty chattered eagerly, clearly excited at the get-together.

It will just be all the more beautiful when it comes, she said as he slid into the bench across from them.

It better be, Kim said as she worked her belly down into the booth next to him.

I think it will, Mo offered hopefully. Anyway, for now, let's warm up with some coffee. She turned over the remaining two upside-down cups on the table and filled them from the carafe the waitress had left. For the next hour, the breakfast conversation was filled with equal portions of the standard "Where are you from / What do you do / How are your eggs" nonsense, and when they exited the diner, the morning was still a cold one. Marty and Kim embraced, and began one of those lengthy goodbyes in which the female of the species is often wont to engage. Mo and Elroy looked at each other with a shared, mild annoyance in their eyes.

So you're heading back uptown? Elroy asked.

Yeah, I guess I am. I don't have much going on today.

No class?

Fuck that.

I'll probably just head up to the library and do some reading.

Sounds cozy.

Elroy smirked. Mo took it seriously.

It's warm in the winter and cool in the summer. Not a bad place to hole up in from time to time.

Gotcha. Hey listen man... I don't get out so much now that Kim's pregnant and all, but what do you say we find a night to get together and shoot some pool?

I can dig it.

Elroy was punching Mo's number into his phone just as the women were returning their attention to them. Kim spoke.

I'm so glad we finally met! Marty talks about you at work all the time.

Mo smiled.

That's disconcerting. Elroy, gimme a call one of these nights. We'll do it up.

You got it. It was good meeting you, even if I don't hear about you at work all the time.

They all laughed, Marty somewhat sheepishly so. She kissed Mo on the cheek, told him she'd see him see him at home later that night, and then she crossed the street with Kim and Elroy, heading for the downtown 1/9 train. Mo watched them for a moment, and suddenly realized that it really was a cold spring day. *Jesus, it's gotta be in the fucking 30s. And it looks like it might rain later too.* He threw up the hood of his sweatshirt and turned his back to the wind. The early morning rush was still on, and although the sidewalk was mobbed with people bustling to work, Mo felt sheltered from the unpleasant tumult. *I'll see you at home, she said.* Home. It was a word he hadn't heard in quite some time. Not since he was a child, and his mother used to tell him, before he left for school in the morning, to *Oye, mijo, I'll see you after work. Buzz el súper when you get home from school, okay?* And he would be there, at home, waiting for her to finish her shift at Kennedy Fried Chicken so she could come home, fix him a bowl of cereal, and tell him bedtime stories. Suddenly, Mo felt very distant and alone. He loved his childhood, but now, shored up by the waves of years passed, he could face their history and see how simple and yet so difficult it really was. He knew now that his mother never shared a bowl of cereal with him at night to make sure that there would be enough for him to have for breakfast in the morning. He knew that the powdered milk, which she mixed up for the cereal, was highly diluted with water. And he knew that the kites he and the other kids on the block would fly off the roof of his building were little more than leftover plastic bodega bags on a leash. But the neighborhood kids would sneak up onto the roof just the same and send up the kites, which they piloted as if they were the expensive G.I. Joe Sky Striker jets advertized on the commercials. Sometimes, a little neighborhood hottie, a girl named Nancy Blanca, would haul her fighter kite all the way up from 119th and St. Nick up to fly with them. It was during one of those dogfighting days that a little kid named Nicolás made his first and only appearance up on the roof. One arm and one of his legs had been withered from polio since he was a baby, and he used a crutch, which made the stairs of the walkup all but insurmountable. For some time, he silently watched the makeshift kites soar and dive with large, brown, wistful eyes. Finally, he approached our group: *Oye vatos,* he said. *Lemme try.* One of the pilots, a fat, grabastic kid named Kique, ordered him off with the cruelty of childhood: *Pinche puta, how'd you get up here anyway? ¡Vete cabrón!* Nicolás turned away, but Mo called out to him. *Oye broder,* he said. *Try this.* He handed him the string to his own hand-made contraption, whose plastic bag skin was so loose that it vibrated and buzzed in flight. But within a few minutes, Nicolás was the envy of every kid on the roof. For once, the guys took their eyes off Nancy's developing body and looked up in awe as Nicolás—with his one good hand—had the kite sweeping and diving through the sky. Eventually, most of the other kites began to come apart and fall to the ground, but for the longest time, that little kid felt like the King of Washington Heights, and he was happy.

Now, though, the word kite no longer referred to a light frame craft covered with plastic and designed to be flown in the air at the end of a long string. These days, when Mo heard about someone with a kite, it meant they'd just gotten a note from a friend or family member currently doing time at Rikers. Yes, home was a good thing. But it was good thing he hadn't experienced as anything more than a melancholy recollection in quite some time.

Eventually, Mo got that call from Elroy. The next weekend, in fact. He was sitting on a futon in the mulicolored living room which he now shared with Marty when his cell phone rang.

Mo, what's happening, man?

Nada. Nada damn thing, really.

So are you still up to shoot a little stick?

Most definitely, man. You got a place you like to play? What about that spot on West 21st near where Kim and Marty work?

That swanky ass place? Nah, man, it's too much like a club. Actually, there's a bar way uptown I heard about, sorta near the University, in fact. Their team won the city championship last year.

You mean the Twilight Lounge?

Yeah. I always wanted to check that place out.

We could do that. You know where it's at?

It's on 106th and Amsterdam, right? I'll just take the train up to 103rd. See you there at, say, ten?

Ten, yeah. I'll see you there.

Mo slapped his cell phone shut and leaned back in the futon. *Why would he want to go all the way uptown? The place isn't even that well known. It's basically just an old school local hangout . . .* He looked at his watch. Eight fifteen. *Might as well leave now, and get a slice on the way.*

The Twilight Lounge was located on a shady stretch of Amsterdam Avenue, just north of the Frederick Douglass projects. But the neighborhoods in this part of Manhattan were changing fast. Just as the University was pushing its way up Broadway and on into Harlem, the Upper West Side was expanding into the Dominican and Puerto Rican neighborhood of Manhattan Valley. It was as if a great, white, gentrifying glacier was slowly forcing its way up the island, retracing ancient, geologic steps, and swallowing up the smaller ethnic neighborhoods like unwanted boulders in its path. For the time being, though, the red neon lights above the door shone out into the night as if it were a lighthouse signaling the existence of an authentic remnant of soon-to-be days gone by.

Mo stood outside the lounge, smoking a cigarette and waiting for Elroy to show. Just as he took his last drag, and exhaled a lungfull of smoke into the cold spring night, Elroy stepped around the corner.

I didn't know you smoked?

It happens.

I can't believe you're waiting outside. It's fucking cold. C'mon man, let's go inside.

The "lounge"—more of a darkened, one-room dive, really—was defined by the bar up front and the lone pool table in the back. The white plaster ceiling was stained with smoke from the days before the new mayor enacted the citywide ban on cigarettes in bars. The table was currently occupied, so Mo and Elroy bellied up to the empty bar to wait their turn.

Damn, it feels good to get out of the house, even for a bit. I've turned into a fucking hermit since the pregnancy was in its second trimester.

I can't even imagine. So does she get insane cravings and shit?

She always has to have fat free milk in the fridge, and decaf coffee. But mostly she's become obsessed with Heinz 57 sauce. She even puts it on spaghetti.

You've got to be fucking kidding me. But seriously though, you got any names on the short list?

If it's a boy, she wants to name him Emre.

Family name?

Nah, after the restaurant we had our first date at.

Mo smiled. He hadn't been in this bar in some time, but being back lent him a sense of warmth. He ordered a shot of Jameson and a pint of Murphy's Irish Stout. The bartender, a full Irish national, grinned. *A Jamie and a Murphy coming up...*

Pretty fucking romantic.

Yo lemme ask you a question. You interested in doing a little partying tonight?

Mo looked him in the eyes for a long, hard moment. They were the thin, oblique eyes that are so often able to draw out a desired response from certain types of men like a poultice. But he doubted very much that Elroy had ever used them to elicit something from a man such as him, and that made him skeptical.

I don't think so.

Hey, I'm not going to be talking to Kim and Marty about it, if that's what you're worried about. I'm just looking to get out of the fucking apartment and cut loose a little bit.

That's not it.

But you know where to go for it, right? I've got the money...

Mo was starting to get a bit agitated.

Course I know where to fucking get it. If you were the partying sort, then you'd know where you get your shit too.

Elroy blinked.

Look man, I apologize. I'm not trying to put you out of sorts or anything. I was just asking. You know, as a favor.

Sorry, I just can't swing it tonight.

I understand.

He looked away.

Anyway, you still up for some pool? I'll throw some quarters down on the table…

The rest of the night passed without incident, but the next morning, Mo told Marty about it. They were in bed, the cold spring sun was filtering in through the window, and though it was early, they both knew that Marty would be late for work that morning. They hunkered down underneath the comforter, laughing as they explored each other's bodies with legs, fingers, noses, and lips, only to fall voiceless when Mo felt her weight on top of him, felt her settle into his arms, and her hair hung soft and loose and warm about his face. Marty almost always pulled her hair back before going to bed, but for some reason, this morning it was free and tangled and tousled, and when she shook her head it fell over him like a spice. After the culmination of their morning love, Marty looked at him through a few strands of that hair and said,

In our life together, will every morning feel as warm as this one? Even if when it's cold outside?

Yes. Even if when it's cold outside.

She sighed contentedly.

Did you and Elroy have fun last night?

I guess so. Yeah.

What does that mean?

Well…

Mo was never ceased to be amazed by how quickly the subject could change when it came to conversation with a woman.

He asked about scoring some coke.

And you said no?

'Course I said no.

But you wanted to?

No. It was nothing. Simple as that.

Marty looked up at the window. Mo already knew what was coming next.

Are you into that stuff at all? I mean, I'm not trying to be judgmental or anything. I just want to know.

You want to know…

I mean, I'd like to know. I'd like to know you, that's all.

Baby it's okay. It's fine. Let's just say I've had some experience with that sort of thing. It's kind of hard not to up in that neighborhood. It's everywhere. There are clockers on every goddamn block.

That's all I wanted to know. You don't have to explain. Not to me, anyway. I just like knowing you, like I said. That's all.

She slid closer to him in the bed, drawn as if iron to a magnet, twining her leg around his, and for a very brief moment Mo thought that the sound of the soft coo escaping her pursed lips was not unlike that of a mourning dove. He closed his eyes against the cold spring sun raining down upon them through the bedroom window.

A month passed. It was April now though still cold, still damp, the North Woods still smelling of roots and soil even as the beautiful spring which he had forecasted was growing ever nearer. One such afternoon found Mo lounging around the apartment reading the *Daily News,* when the door blew open and Marty blustered in, home early from work.

Hey. Listen, Kim and Elroy are having a party at their apartment this weekend.

Rock on.

But there's something I need to talk to you about first...

She hung her messenger's bag over a chair, sat down, and turned to face Mo, who was on the couch across from her.

We're supposed to bring something to the party.

I can pick up some cachaça at the liquor store on First. You know, make some caipirinhas. Everybody likes caipirinhas, right?

That's not it.

What are you talking about?

Mo was suddenly skeptical. Marty took in a breath.

Party favors.

Judas fucking priest...

Baby don't get mad. Just listen a second. Of course Kim's not going to be partying. But Elroy wants to, and she's okay with that. And you said you had some experience with that sort of thing...

And?

And I kinda thought about partying a little bit too.

I knew it. I fucking knew it.

Is that bad?

Mo could only laugh.

That depends on how bad you want it.

Now Marty was indignant.

Look, they're friends of ours. And last time I checked, we didn't have a lot of friends to go out and have fun with. This is what people do, Mo. They go out and have fun and party together.

But Kim's fucking pregnant!

And I said she's not partying. She'll have a glass of red wine, if that. And so what if they're about to start a family? If anything, that earns them the right to a night out and about. And you know what?

Mo knew, all right. But she answered her own question for him.

It might be good for you, too, you know. You've been a little withdrawn, lately...

Fine. All right? Fine. Whatever you say.

Baby...

But Mo had already grabbed his cell phone and was cycling through the numbers. Marty could hear the ring on the other end until Mo put the phone up to his ear and turned away to face the window.

¿Quiubo que más? It's Mo. Yeah man I need some llello for this weekend, can you hook me up? Cien, como siempre. Aiight broder. Thank you.

He clapped his cell phone shut. Without turning to look at Marty, he said,

There. We're all set. Okay?

Marty leapt up from her seat and kissed him on the nose.

You're such a sucker for love, she said, smiling, as if she'd just performed a magic trick.

Saturday came. Mo left the apartment early so he could pick up the party favors. When he got to the foyer, he dialed a number into his phone, spoke a few words, and then hung up. A few minutes later, a black Lincoln town car pulled up to the curb outside. It looked every bit like a licensed New York City limousine, save for the telltale "T" on the license plate. Mo exited the building, opened the door, and ducked into the back seat of the car. As it pulled back into traffic, the passenger in the front seat turned around and grinned. It was one of Kingston's men. They slapped hands.

Never less than a hundo, right cabrón?

You know it.

Mo handed over five twenty-dollar bills, and the front seat passenger passed him the twisted up bag of cocaine.

Pleasure doing business with you.

Always, mi broder.

The town car drove around for a few more blocks, just to make the pick-up look like a legitimate fare. When they dropped Mo off back at the apartment, Marty was dressed and ready. The party Kim and Elroy were throwing turned out to be a birthday party for one of their publishing friends, an editor at an adult male magazine. Dozens of well-dressed men and women were milling about along the pumpkin-colored walls and fashionably sipping demi-sec champagne. Mo noticed that the only other man in the room wearing a t-shirt was still more stylish than he was: it was a V-neck. Suddenly, Elroy materialized out of the crowd and gave him a hug.

I'm fired up that you made it, man. Marty tells me we're going to be partying a little bit tonight!

Really? Well if she said so...

Elroy laughed and thumped him on the shoulder.

That's what I like about you, bro. You know how to roll with it, you know how to adapt! But first things first... what do you want a drink?

With drinks in hand, the foursome made the standard, slow circle of the room, the way a dog turns circles before feeling secure enough with a place to settle down to sleep in the midst of it. Mo felt very much like the odd man out—felt like every eye at the party was focused on him—and as they made their rounds, he avoided encounters and spoke very little. He knew it was just a case of his social paranoia, but nevertheless, he couldn't remember having felt this uncomfortable since the sexually charged parties with professors and grad students up at the University. He was being accosted by a *New York Post* gossip columnist when Elroy grabbed his arm and pulled him to safety.

Man, I don't know about you, but I need a bump. Let's find the commode in this dungeon.

Mo was too distressed by the whole production to argue this point any further. He nodded appreciatively at Elroy and sidled his way through the crowd towards the bathroom, which he had passed at some point during his social revolutions. Ignoring any semblance of modesty, they both entered the bathroom together and locked the door behind them. Mo pulled the tiny ziploc bag containing the gram of coke out of his pocket, and Elroy pulled out his keychain.

You first, he said, handing the keys to Mo.

Mo laid the bag flat on the sink and gently began to crush up the soft, gypsum-like crumbles into a finer powder. Then he pinched the edges of the bag between his left thumb and forefinger, separating the flaps at the top. With his right hand, he dug one of the keys into the powdered contents, scooped out a bump, and snorted it up one nostril. He rubbed his nose, feeling it drip down the back of his throat, and passed the bag to Elroy.

Damn baby, Elroy said after taking a bump of his own. That's some good shit you've got!

They returned to the party, bright-eyed and verbose, and stepped back into the collective dervish of a crowd. They schmoozed with an off-Broadway actor, then a screenwriter, then an off-duty photographer, before finding themselves back with Kim and Marty again. When Marty saw that they were still carrying around the same, unsipped drinks from before, she knew what they had been doing instead. She turned and cozied up to Mo, brushing her denim-clad derriere ever so slightly against Mo's hips, and whispered,

Is it my turn yet?

Mo stealthily pulled out the bag and slid it into her back pocket. Then she kissed him on the ear and headed off to the bathroom herself.

During the course of the party, the three of them finished off the gram, while Kim stuck fastidiously to her ginger ale and cranberry juice. It was two in the morning by the time that Marty and Mo left the party, and the frigid night air—combined with the comedown from the earlier high—left Marty shivering nervously. When they finally arrived back at the apartment, they dove half-clothed into bed together, nuzzling under the comforter, and made love aimlessly until dawn, when Mo finally rolled over into an overdue and much needed sleep.

Spring eventually did arrive, and it was as recognizable as an old, ritualistic train that had fallen just a few minutes behind schedule, as if hearkening the odd convergence of time and space that takes place when the last train leaving the station meets with the first light of day. The cold winter rain continued, but now it fell in a soft screen upon the tiny green buds of tulip trees and little leaf lindens, who were finally willing to offer up their flowers to the city. The North Woods Ravine, being the only true valley in the Park, was filling with runoff, and the stream swelled and churned and rolled upon itself before crashing down the waterfall into the Loch. But Mo bore no witness to the changes in his old, fraternal woodland, for he had not visited it since moving in with Marty.

It was on one such spring day that a card arrived in her mailbox. Since Mo was in the apartment most afternoons while Marty was at work, he was there when the mail arrived. The envelope was stout, textured bond paper sealed with a blue bow, and it was addressed to the both of them. The return address, he recognized, was that of Kim and Elroy. Mo opened the envelope and pulled out the card inside:

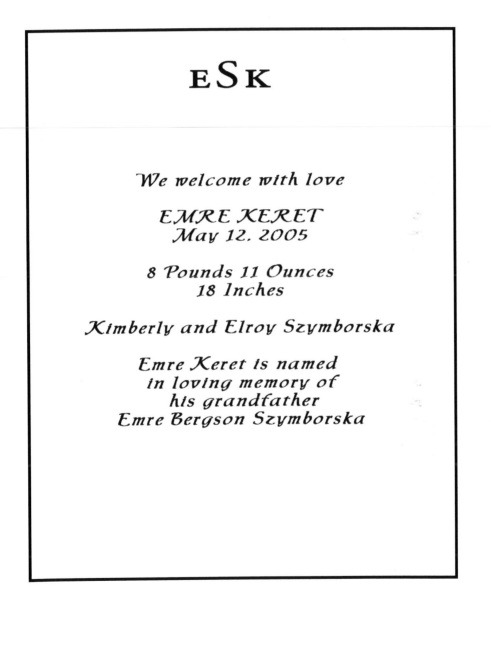

E S K

We welcome with love

EMRE KERET
May 12, 2005

8 Pounds 11 Ounces
18 Inches

Kimberly and Elroy Szymborska

Emre Keret is named
in loving memory of
his grandfather
Emre Bergson Szymborska

Mo spent a few minutes wondering about the various names and measurements before placing the card and its envelope on the small end table near the door. When Marty returned to the apartment later that evening, she noticed the card laying there even before she tossed her keys on the table. Her gut knew what it said before her eyes could confirm it.

Wow! I have to call them, or email... I mean, I have to call them and tell them to email some pictures! Oh my God, this is wonderful! This is so, so wonderful...

All of a sudden, she seemed breathless, as if reading the card was as invigorating as sprinting down the block after a departing bus. She sat down on the couch without having taken off her coat. The card was still in her hand, but her eyes were looking up and away while her chest rose and fell with deep, repeated breaths. Slowly, her excitement seemed to give way to a silent, aching sadness. Unsure of what to do, Mo offered up a meaningless question.

Great name they picked, eh?

Marty sighed.

It sounds like Henry...

Henry?

I love the name Henry. For a baby, I mean. I don't know why. I just always have.

Is it an old family name or something?"

No, it's just the sound of the name, it always reminded me...

Her voice was more hushed now, almost approaching a whisper.

Sometimes when I'm at work I'll get takeout for lunch and go sit on a bench in Madison Square Park. You know? Just to watch the birds.

You go there and what, feed the pigeons?

No, not the pigeons. I just like watching the little birds there. The ones that remind me of Lake George... the ones I hope I'll see up at the hotel when I start the job up there this season.

Well, if they're there in the park, I'm sure they're going to be up-state too...

There's this baby wren that likes to perch up on top of a humming-bird feeder and just bask in the afternoon sun...

Her eyes seemed to be looking at something astronomically distant.

Baby what are you talking about?

It's such a precious looking thing... bigger than I thought it would be by now, but with a beak and wings that still aren't fully formed. It looks so very soft and so very afraid... it's head is always moving, and if I didn't know better I'd think it was lost. But I know it's not... I've watched it enough to have seen its nest there, just a few feet away, in a basket of flowers hanging from one of the streetlights. Sometimes, I'll even stop in the park after work, before I come home. That's when you can hear the katydids buzzing around, and you can sit there on the park bench and watch the mother flittering out from the nest and go looking for food. I've seen it bring back almost everything—grubs, crickets, even spiders from time to time—and as soon as the baby feels its mother near, you can hear it starting to squeak with joy...

Mo's eyes began to steel themselves, not in anger, but as a means of bracing himself for the profundity of what was to come. *It has already happened to her. And now it is about to happen to me. Wait for it, wait for it, for it is coming...*

But he could not.

How long has it been?

Sixteen days.

Are you sure? Mo asked her this, though he was really talking only to himself. Sometimes women are late, right? I mean, you can't really be sure until...

Do you really believe that?

Then—as her voice fell even more faint—she replaced the rhetorical question with a supremely real one.

Do you want a baby?

Remember when I said you are a gift?

Yes.

I meant that. I meant that you are a gift to me. But a baby... a baby would a gift to the both of us. *A gift we give to ourselves, a gift bought and paid for with some combination of human love and genetic codes, with the roilings of life and passion, the vicissitudes of what might even save us in the end.*

That makes me happy.

It makes me happy too.

Mo wanted to ask her about a doctor, but knowing that her first pregnancy ended in a miscarriage, he decided against it. *There will be so many things to plan, so many decisions to make, so many changes to experience...* Marty cut off his train of thought with a surprising change of subject.

Do you remember up at the Lake? When I asked you how you could trust me? How you could trust in me, even after what I did?

Yes.

And you remember what you said?

Yes.

You healed me that morning.

It was the truth. It was the truth that did that.

But it hurts now. I knew it... I knew the euphoria wouldn't last...

Euphoria doesn't matter when the love is there. And it will be. Always. Love is a constant. I promise you.

No... it's fading already... what have I done?

Baby calm down... just take a deep breath and take it easy...

No no no no...

Talk to me... Marty what's going on? Just tell me...

You weren't the only one.

Suddenly, Mo felt disemboweled.

Marty what the hell are you saying?

I called him. I called Junior. The night before I asked you that question. I went out on a walk in the woods and I called him.

What did you say?

Marty was staring at the floor, and standing as still as the air on an Iowa afternoon just before a hailstorm.

I told him where I was...

And?

And he said he used to go camping near there. With his brother.

Go on, Mo said. But be very, very careful. The truth. Now.

Marty began to cry.

I saw him once after we went back to the city. Just to talk. He told me he wanted me to come back. I just felt so sick. It was like I didn't know what to do, but even if I did, I wouldn't be able to do it. Not the right thing, anyway...

But you did something.

I thought if I asked you to move in with me, that everything else would just go away. God how did I become this sort of person?

Just keep talking.

Marty wiped her eyes and looked at him long enough to see that there was nothing in his. Absolutely nothing. Every emotion human beings can feel had in a single, microscopic moment been burned away, leaving nothing but the barren plain and charred bones of his soul. She continued.

I told him no. And he said okay. He let me say no, but he told me that I could come back. That I could always come back. And after awhile, that became the only thing that mattered. The fact that I could always go back. And I did.

Mo's face was starting to show some emotion now. The edges of his eyelids were starting to turn red.

When? When did you go back to him? For how long? How many times? Tell me. Tell me now.

We went to the Warwick.

No...

I had to figure out a way to know for sure. I had to. And if I could go back to him there, at our hotel, then I would know...

Don't ever fucking say that. Don't ever use the word "our" again.

Mo...

Wait. Just wait a minute. You started this whole thing by asking me if I wanted a baby. And what did I say?

I know what you said.

I said a baby would be a wonderful gift to us. Didn't I?

Yes.

But it's not mine, is it?

How could I have done this... .

I know it's not mine because I always played it safe. But you knew where you were going with this, didn't you? You knew you could always go back to him, and you knew you would never leave a baby behind. Am I right? Whether you knew it or not, that was your plan. Don't even bother responding. Just tell me this: what kind of man would let you live with someone else all this time and just wait for you to eventually come back to him?

Someone who's just as much of a broken mess as me.

You're right. You're motherfucking right about that. You treacherous fucking bitch.

Mo was surprised by the purity of his own distilled vitriol. It was something he'd never felt before in his life, but it would stay with him for many, many years to come. There was nothing hot blooded in his anger; in fact, it was more of an iron-like frigidity, a moribund cold, one more aspic than icy, and all the worse because of it. He felt scarcely able to breathe (let alone live) and what scared him the most was that he didn't even care. It was a tragedy, of course, but this feeling was something with which he would become profoundly intimate, something that would leave an ineffaceable scar upon the soul, something that would forever occupy the same place in his memory as his first experience with both sex and the drawing of another man's blood. The way that Judas Iscariot occupied the incontrovertible jaws of Satan together with Brutus and Cassius. *They say that Hell is separation from God's love and warmth. I don't believe in God, but I know what cold feels like and now I know what it feels like to be frozen neck-deep in Cocytus, too.*

There were very few things left to say after that. Mo left the apartment, taking only his jacket, and began walking uptown. It would be a long walk, but he would need every step of the way to realize just how far astray he'd gone because of an illusion. The French have a saying, On va bien loin depuis qu'on est las, but that all depends on what a man thinks he's going to get in the end. *A house in the mountains. Amber dawns and azure evenings and clear night skies unpolluted by city lights. The unconditional love of a woman. That's what I went all in for. And I just went bankrupt.* That much was clear, but with every passing step, Mo began to wonder whether he had gambled on love with Marty, or whether he'd bet it all on the existence of love itself. He tried hard to think, to reason, to rationalize. But with each passing block, he became more and more aware of the fact that he truly did not know, he did not know whether love could ever exist in a capricious world where even the Wildflower Meadow, resting on the slopes of the Ravine on the most sun-dappled of days, could be undone by a sudden wind and a fast-moving cloud. *And so this is the worst of it: the not knowing. Not knowing what love is, not knowing what it might be, not even knowing what it ever was.* As he walked, he searched for words to describe this sensation of overwhelming doubt—tried to distract himself by trying to explain it all—but it was next to impossible. *Awful? No, there is no awe in this whatsoever. Terrible? Horrible? Doubt can cause terror, horror, and fear, but it also does nothing to explain it. No. It is a disappearance. A void. A vanishing. An abduction. And then it just goes on from there. But I do know one thing,* he thought, his stomach finally calming somewhat. *It's fucking cold outside, and I need to find someplace warm.*

A few blocks later, he found himself in front of the familiar neon lights of the Lion's Den. From the outside looking in, Mo could only discern five silhouettes inside, plus the bartender, but when he entered, they were the five he wanted to see: Mike, Hook, Black Jay, Fabian, and Ozone.

Jesus Mo, you look like a talent agent for a fucking graveyard, man.

Mo gratefully accepted a lager from Dos Jotas, and proceeded to describe the evening's events in no small amount of terms. Fabian let out a low whistle.

Bone of your bone, dude. Bone of your bone.

Yeah, Mo answered. That's about it.

Gradually, his friends paid their tabs and left, but Mo and Fabian continued to drink until last call. Even then, after the outer gates were lowered and the neon lights were turned off, Dos Jotas continued to fill their glasses a few more times as he was totaling the register receipts. When he finished closing up, he came around to the other end of the bar, sat down, and took out a sack of weed and a blunt. He split the blunt down the middle, shook out the tobacco, and replaced it with the entire bag of weed before rolling it back up, licking it, and sealing it up with his lighter. He took a long drag on it himself before passing it over to Mo, who took a puff as well. They smoked in silence for a minute or two before Fabian offered up a thought.

Listen man, I know this is some fucked up shit, but lemme tell you what I think about it. It wasn't your fault that you fell for her. It wasn't even her fault that she fell for you, either. It's never love's fault. You can't say, "I loved her too much" or any of that bullshit. So don't blame it on that. What happened was that she just didn't deserve the chance to truly love. Not with you, and not with this Junior guy. She lost the right to do that. She had her chance and she missed it. The crazy thing is, neither of you ever even considered that it might not work. This guy Junior knew both sides of the story, and he's the only one who saw the end result coming.

Has he ever come in here since the night I met them?

I've never seen him since then.

Man. Why did this ever have to happen. Why did it even have to start.

You want to hear my theory on that?

Nah, man. You turn into one verbal ass motherfucker when you're fucked up.

Dos Jotas laughed.

You wanna break out the PlayStation? Play some Madden on the TV in the back room for awhile?

Nah, bro. But thanks. I'm gonna roll on back to the crib.

Aiight man. You do what you gotta do. Take it easy. And stay up, player. Always stay up. Just keep your dick hard and your powder dry, and the world will turn. The world will turn.

They slapped hands, and Mo and Fabian stepped out the heavy side door onto 109th Street. The cool night air in his face sobered him up just a bit. He pulled an old pack of Parliaments from of his jacket pocket, shook one out, and lit it. Fabian lit up a cowboy killer.

You sure you're alright man? We could roll back up to my place. You know, download some Metallica and kick out the jams. Whaddaya think?

I'm fine. I'm just gonna roll home and put this day out of its misery.

Whatever man. Va fa Napoli.

This ain't Rome, homes.

Fabian laughed, tossed his cigarette in the gutter, and started walking up Amsterdam toward his own apartment. If you say so, he said. Mo looked around the intersection, finishing his smoke. One of King's clockers was across the street. Mo nodded at him, and he came over. A few seconds later, Mo was on his way home for the first time in months with a half a gram of blow in his pocket.

Mo was up all night doing lines off a plastic CD case, forcing some sort of elation into his soul despite the fact that there was no real joy in his life to draw upon. But it worked for a time, this artificial delectation, and Mo laid there on the couch awash in it, feeling as elevated, as positive, as expectant, and as sexually excited as he could remember having felt in the arms of a woman. *After all, it's all just a matter of the glands, right? Food, sex, love, fighting, dopamine, nicotine, amphetamines. It doesn't matter what it is, or where it comes from. It's all just about feeling good...*

But of course it wasn't all just about feeling good. Mo knew that. He knew that you can find pleasure in many things, but they all involve the same sort of collapse. Some form of disintegration. Love is a high, and betrayal is a fall from grace. Alcohol or other drugs can draw you out of your depression, but they charge a high price for their services. Gradually, each additional line felt less uplifting, and Mo knew his ride was coming to an end even before he snorted his last little bit. By the time the coke was gone, the come-down was already in full swing. Mo leaned back, longing for sleep or alcohol or a cigarette or anything else that could turn this plummeting around or at least slow it somewhat. But he knew that nothing was coming. There was nothing to do but lay back and face the paranoia that comes from having nothing to look forward to save for the absolute worst-case scenario.

I see her... I can see Marty there. Sitting on the floor with a child. A little boy, less than a year old. Go, she's saying, Go to Daddy... and the boy giggles, pounds his tiny palms on the carpet, and eagerly crawls across the room towards his father with the sort of excited delight that belongs perhaps only to children… his father leans down to receive him, to pick him up and plop him down on his knee, kisses his innocent fuzzy head, and turns to look back at Marty. I wonder if love or something like love exists between them, or if this vision of things to come is simply the product of the physical machinations conducted by the flesh in an attempt to create artificial desire out of nothingness. For the child's sake, I hope it's the former. I hope that for him. Because we have blundered our way through his life—leaving betrayal and deception and forgiveness and reconciliation as our footprints—and where I come from, the sins of the father are not visited upon the son. There is enough suffering in life without the need for any compounding, because who among us knows if we were born stout and strong and decent enough to be able to endure either suffering or love? And if that is the case, perhaps I have no right to hope. Perhaps the best I can do is wish it. Wish that justice and righteousness will give way to consolation and peace.

Two weeks later, his cell phone rang. It was Kingston.

Big Mo, you back in the neighborhood?

Yeah man, why what's up?

I heard you were back. And I heard why. I heard about all that shit.

Glad to know the word is out.

Listen mi broder, for what it's worth, I get it. There's a reason I'm not with my girl's mother anymore.

I know that too. How is she anyway?

She's back with her grandmama.

That's good.

Yeah bro. She misses things already. She digs the swings at the Anibal Aviles Playground, but she's getting bigger now and sometimes I catch her watching the pickup games on the court across the street at Booker T. Washington. She wants to ball, she's all into the WNBA now, you know?

She's a superstar.

Listen, are you back at your rig right now? I got something I want to talk to you about.

Mo told him that he was, and Kingston said he would come by in a short while. He didn't say what for, but to Mo it didn't much matter in the face of everything else. *It's probably his piece,* he figured. *He needs it back now that his daughter's left.* With the help of a chair, Mo retrieved it from its hiding place in the coat closet and placed it on the top shelf of his bookcase. When Kingston called up from the street a little less than an hour later, Mo buzzed him in. They embraced.

What up King? I've got your piece for you. Haven't even touched it since the last time you were here.

Kingston looked at him.

Thank you man. But that's not why I'm here. Yo, sit down for a minute.

Mo suddenly felt a bit unnerved. He didn't owe him any money, and he didn't know anybody who did. But he sat down on the off-yellow couch next to Kingston anyway, because he needed to.

Listen man, I know times is rough right now, so I got something to distract you a little bit. You know, get your mind focused back to reality, you know what I'm saying?

Not yet I don't.

Let me put it to you this way...

Kingston reached down one leg of his pants and withdrew a plastic sandwich bag tightly twisted around a hackey-sack sized lump of white powder. He gently laid it down on the coffee table in front of them. Mo stared at it, transfixed. In the fluorescent light of the room, the contents of the bag shone like a giant pearl.

Is that what I think it is?

Fishscale, motherfucker.

So what's it got to do with me?

This is your shot, man. This is your new motherfucking direction.

What are you talking about?

Look, here's the situation... I need to get this to a client down in Central Jersey this weekend, and it can't go on the train. Since 9/11, they've got dogs sniffing all over Penn Station.

Take my car...

You know I got no license. If I get pulled over, se acabo, man. Se acabo.

Drive the speed limit, bro. Use your fucking turn signal, for Christ's sake...

Nah man, you don't get it. It's not about being legit. I mean, look at me. The Jersey jakes will pull me over just on profiling alone. But you got light skin, you got no tats on your neck. You're fucking pristine, man. You're good to go. You're good to fucking go.

You want me to move this weight.

That's it, broder. Like they say, cook the shake and move the weight across the Tri-State.

So what's in it for me?

The client pays you fifteen hundred. You keep five, and bring the grand back to me. All in a day's work. So what you thinking?

What do I think. That's a hell of a question. I think the money matters. I think it might offer me a way to start over. A chance at redemption, or maybe just retribution. When you think about it, there's not that much of a difference, really. But there's danger in it as well. Money is a human construct, but it has a life of its own. It's a real, honest to God Frankenstein's monster. Like a politician, no matter how benevolent, who — once elected — enacts a law that keeps him in office. And once you let it into your life, you become dependant on it. It's not all that different from love in that sense. What good is love if it doesn't offer security? But what good is an agreement if nobody's making any money? It may not bring happiness, but it sure as hell can take away any worries you might have about your future. If nothing else, it's a chance to start over, a chance to get in a whole new fucking game. And to play that fucking game for keeps. Mo thought about how he'd anted up and invested before — once for a chance at higher education, and then again for a chance at love — and how he'd lost big on both fronts. But there, carefully considering the cost of the love he had once felt so truly and purely like some sort of divine accountant, Mo could find no reason why not to take on this new economic risk that had been laid out in front of him. It was as inevitable and deadly as a deer caught in the headlights of a speeding car.

Just give me the goddamn details, bro.

It goes down Saturday. One o'clock. Princeton Junction. Early that morning, you drive on down; there's this Chinese restaurant there, called Happy Family, right near the train station on the Northeast Corridor line. Park there, honk three times, and then wait for your phone to ring.

That's it?

That's it, man.

Kingsston stood up. Mo stood up with him. They slapped hands and embraced. When they withdrew, Kingston had a big, leering grin on his face.

You my pinche pana now, son! ◆

The Lantern

OR THE NEXT FEW MONTHS, Al and Willie saw each other nearly every day, though the kiss was never repeated. Sunday brunch at the Dean became a standing date for them, though they never again returned to Utopia. They spent the rest of their time out and about in the neighborhood. They strolled among the cherry trees and ambled past Shakespearean foliage at the Botanical Gardens. They stood alongside immense, philosophic bronze and marble sculptures during the Auguste Rodin exhibit at the Brooklyn Museum. They spent one quiet, springtime afternoon lazily strolling up and down the full two miles of Eastern Parkway's tree-lined boulevard, and another one jumping and dancing as the raucous West Indian Day Parade traversed that same stretch of road in the fall. But what they both liked most about the neighborhood was its proximity to Prospect Park.

Willie preferred it to Central Park, finding it more rugged and bucolic than its more famous Manhattan counterpart, many parts of which reminded him, rather annoyingly, of a well manicured golf course. Some years ago, he spent a great deal of time there, but since his arrival in Brooklyn, Prospect Park had become much more of a treasure to him. It was a land-locked and self-contained world of greenery and waterways that screened out any signs of external buildings or traffic, a seemingly limitless wilderness within the city itself. To him, Central Park might well be the Vatican City of New York, walled in by skyscrapers eternally threatening incursions, giving the whole 800-odd acres the feeling of an enclave, a lockaway claustrum within the city itself. But in Brooklyn they could have badminton picnics on the Long Meadow, they could dance to free concerts at the bandshell, and they even could even ride horses with a man named Cecil Stokes, one of the Black Cowboys who operated out of the Kensington Stables. But by far and away, the thing they loved the most were the pedal boats. Their standard strategy was to pick a day when Al had no apartments to show, and could instead meet Willie at the diner after his morning shift. From there they would walk along Washington Avenue past the Brooklyn Museum, past Medgar Evers College, until they reached the confluence of Flatbush, Lincon Road, and Ocean Avenue. From there, it was an easy walk to the ice skating rink, where the pedal boats were rented. It was just after noon; the sun was high and the surface of the lake was free from water lilies and algae. Al and Willie strapped on their orange life vests and boarded their vessel, side by side.

You pedal first.

Al smiled from behind her sunglasses and reclined to the extent that she could in the boat.

Aye, captain. Now shove off! I've got the helm!

Willie set out on a broad, lethargic loop of the lake. First, he steered them around the Peninsula, which jutted out into the lake as if it were Italy in the Mediterranean. At the tip of the boot was a rustic pavilion fashioned from stout, rough-hewn logs. Sitting on the bench there was another young couple, arm in arm, watching their massive rottweiler romping around. Al and Willie waved at them; the young couple waved back. Willie was inspired to muse:

Did you know that ninety percent of all dogs owned in Brooklyn are rottweilers?

Really? I had no idea. I mean, they're so big, for a city dog...

Willie broke out into peals of laughter.

I'm kidding. I totally just made that up.

Al slapped him on his arm.

You just earned yourself another turn at the tiller, sailor!

But Willie was happy to oblige. It was such a peaceful day, after all. It was a weekday, and they were just about the only boat out on the unbroken, glassy water. Lookout Hill was looming perhaps a hundred yards off the port bow. The pass which lay alongside it was once lost to the British by General Washington. Back then, Flatbush was a town, not an avenue, the city was farmland, and you could see the Atlantic Ocean in the distance. Willie's mind began to wander. *It makes you think. About the permanence of things. About how much of the original can withstand the passing of time, the turning of the years. Do writers care whether they publish in a daily newspaper or with a publisher whose books never go out of print? And what about me? What have I done with my life? Have I left any marks upon history, the way the ancient, ineffaceable glaciers left a terminal moraine that would one day become the most western tip of something that would come to be known as Long Island...*

But he was jerked back to reality when Al squealed.

Oh my God! I almost forgot... I saw the funniest thing last night.

What was that?

I was on the 4 train coming home, and when I got off at Franklin Road, I saw this Hassidic guy totally making out with a black tranny hooker!

Now you're just fucking with me. You're still mad that I got you with that rottweiler thing...

Willie, I'm totally serious!

Well then, there's just one thing I can say to that.

What?

Mazel tov, motherfucker! Mazel tov. But I still don't believe you.

It's true!

Well, I hope he came down to the lake for a mikveh afterwards.

What's that mean?

Ah, forget about it. Anyway, it's your turn now to take the helm.

Al agreed, and she took over piloting duties. She plotted a course that took them past the Lullwater Bridge, which was a quite literal description of the passive fluid sitting beneath it. It was so lull, in fact, so affllicted with a sense of quiet calmness, as if the entire lake were a movie on pause, that they could hear the invisible course of the water as it spilled down the Falkill, Ambergill, and Binnenwater in the ravine before welling up near their present location. That inimitable sound of deliberate, irrepressible, falling water was something which Willie had heard twice before and which he would never forget. To Al, though, it hinted at something else.

Does this remind you at all of *Love in the Time of Cholera?*

Willie thought for a moment, as if to establish for himself that no, he hadn't thought of that before. Al attempted to explain herself.

I mean, look over there at the Boathouse...

She pointed towards the Independence, an electric replica of the old steam-powered riverboat that ferried folks around the lake more than a century ago.

Couldn't you just see that thing, I don't know, just chugging ceaselessly up and down the same old river without ever having to call in to port?

I really don't know. The only rivers I've ever seen are the East River, and the Hudson...

But Willie had indeed read that book before, and when he thought about it, he realized that he could, in fact, see that boat there, pulling back from the boathouse, any boathouse, perhaps even an apocryphal Colombian boathouse, and turning upstream, towards La Dorada, embarking on a slow, crawling course up a lackadaisical river, shining like burnished copper in the later afternoon sun, its towering lateral wheel turning in a constant gyre, the engine belching out swollen clouds of steam and smoke, reeking its way through the dense and desolate jungle, churning, diminishing in the distance, shrinking down to the point where it didn't even seem to be moving anymore, having instead become stationary, like an ornament on the invisible Christmas tree of the horizon.

... I guess I can see it, though. It gets cramped and smothering in the city all the time. But not here. This is kind of a release. It feels pretty free and easy out here on the water, actually.

When I was a kid, I always wanted to live near water. And I guess I still do, in a way. It's in my nature. You know what I'd really like, though? I'd like an island all to myself. You know? Just a little island. For getting away. But I guess this is as close as I'm going to get...

What's a guy supposed to say to that? It sounded like resignation, like a confession. But she said it so calmly, so pensively, the way she might dismiss an expected letter that hasn't yet arrived in the mail. It sounds almost like she's become all too familiar with judgment and surrender.

Anyway, you're probably getting hungry by now. We should start heading back to the rink.

After returning the pedal boat, they realized their legs were too spent to walk all the way back up Washington Avenue, so they stood on the corner until they could hail a cab. Seeking a rare change from the Dean, they stopped at Marie Sharp's Belizean Kitchen, where they ordered a humongous plate of red beans and rice topped with red snapper, tomatoes and onions, with a side of roti. Willie did most of the eating, and they boxed up the leftovers to take home with them. After dinner, they stopped at a liquor store for a handle of vodka, and a bottle each of tonic water and cranberry juice. The plan was to go home and watch a movie, but there was nothing on cable, and Al had previously rejected most of Willie's collection of classic films on DVD. The burden was on her, then, to come up with an alternative. After her second cocktail, she had it:

Have you ever done the "Dinner Out" thing?

I thought we already had dinner out tonight…

No, don't be silly. It's an experiment. One of those Gedanken things. Only it's based on a Robert Redford movie.

Oh, you mean one of those ethical tests, right? Where you have to choose one course of action over another?

Yeah, that's it.

Okay, I'm game. So what's the scenario?

Here it is. You're at a bar, drinking with a friend. Your best friend, as a matter of fact, who's like a brother to you. Like your twin brother. As the night goes on, some random stranger insults him. You know, calls him a kike or a nigger or a spic. Something like that. So they go to fight it out into the street, which is totally empty, except for the three of you. Your friend punches the guy, and he goes down hard, hitting his head on the curb, killing him instantly. When the police arrive, they arrest your friend and charge him with murder, and they arrest you as an accomplice. But before the trial, they offer you a deal. Since you are the only witness to what happened, they need your testimony to convict your friend, and in exchange for it, they offer to let you off with probation while he gets ten years for manslaughter. If you refuse to testify, your friend will walk, but you will get convicted of obstruction of justice and go to prison for five years. What do you do?

Willie thought silently for a moment.

Basically, you're asking which quality is more important to me: honesty or friendship.

Pretty much. But either way, one of you does time.

I wonder if she has any idea was that really means: to do time. It just doesn't make sense. Not grammatically, not philosophically. You don't do the time; it's all about what the time does to you.

Well, this isn't exactly Leopold and Loeb. Honestly, after thinking about it, I gotta say I'd chose to not testify.

You'd go to jail to protect a friend?

Yes.

So you think friendship is more important than truth?

Willie paused again, aligning the words to his response in his mind.

I think everyone would agree that being honest would be the morally right thing to do. I mean, you swear an oath to tell the truth, don't you? But the way I see it, friendship is a moral issue too. You can choose to be honest, but you can also choose who your true friends are, and you can choose whether or not to back your brother's play. So, that's what I would do. That's my choice.

Then it was Al's turn to take a contemplative moment.

I'm glad.

About what?

I'm glad you said that. I would choose friendship too, but I like how you said it. It makes more sense to me that way.

Well, you're welcome then.

Can I ask you something else?

Of course.

When you were thinking about your answer, you looked a little... I don't know... I guess it looked like there was a lot going on in there. That you have a lot of reasons for why you answered the way you did.

Willie's voice took on a note of gravity that hadn't been there before.

Let's just say I have a little bit of experience with that sort of thing.

The look in Al's eyes pleaded with him to go on.

There was a time when I would have chosen honesty. Actually, there was a time when I did choose honesty. But it didn't work out the way I thought it would. So now, between honesty and brotherhood, I choose brotherhood.

The pleading look in her eyes was replaced by a knowing one.

It was a girl...

Willie did not respond.

I knew it. From the very first moment we spoke, I knew it. I could hear it in your voice. I can always tell when a person is harboring something by the tone in their voice. So let me guess—and tell me when I'm wrong—you were close with someone, maybe even engaged, but you betrayed her trust about something. Maybe you even cheated on her with someone. And you felt guilty enough to open up and be honest about it, so you told her. And that was it. The end. Am I right?

You'll forgive me if I don't get into details.

Don't worry. I won't hate you. I wouldn't. Not after what happened to my own marriage. I don't care what you might have done. That's your business. All I care about what he did to me.

That's odd. She was wrong about me, but I know how she feels about her ex husband. I know those feelings because I have them too...

You know what else I think?

What's that?

I think you have a little touch of the Hemingway Syndrome.

Willie's eyes opened wide with a combination of surprise and curiosity.

Hemingway Syndrome? What the fuck is that?

It's just a little theory of mine. But see, I think Hemingway's one true love was his first wife Hadley. They fell for each other before any fame or fortune came their way, when they were living in that tiny little apartment in Chicago. But then they moved to France, and it all started to fall apart. He forgave her for losing that manuscript on the train, but he never forgave himself after he betrayed her with that Pfeiffer woman. And he never loved anyone quite like that again. But you know what I think hurt him the most?

What's that?

That she was kind to him all the way up until his death. Even after she remarried, she was still kind and decent to him. And he knew she was a good and true person in that way, and that's why he dedicated his first novel to her and their son.

I always liked that book. I knew a guy from Staten Island once—he was the son of a doctor and a boxing trainer—who described it simply as "a book about a Jew boxer from Princeton." It was the single most concise piece of literary criticism I've ever heard. But I have to admit, Al, I'm a little surprised you know so much about Papa Hem. I mean, considering your own... um... you know, past.

He's the only male author I read. All Faulkner ever wrote were basically soap operas. I pretty much just read the women. But like I said, you've got Hemingway Syndrome, so you probably don't.

Actually, you might be wrong about that.

Oh yeah? Who have you read, then?

Erica Jong.

Al laughed out loud.

Okay, well let me try this from another point of view: you prefer Hemingway to Faulkner, Bogie to Jimmy Stewart, and you like the Stones a hell of a lot more than you like the Beatles.

Well, I do have a "Casablanca" tattoo on my arm...

Al drained her vodka and cranberry and slammed the glass down on the coffee table in astonishment.

No fucking way! Let me see...

Willie pulled up the sleeve of his T-shirt, exposing the ink on his deltoid. Without being asked, he explained:

It's the logo from the side of the French plane at the end of the film.

God, I love that movie. What's your favorite quote?

I like the part when Rick tries to dismiss his sense of idealism by saying he got well paid for it.

I like the part when he warns the Germans about the dangers of invading New York.

Well we invaded it, didn't we? At least this little corner of Brooklyn.

Yes. Yes we did.

Al paused for a long moment. Willie was about to offer to mix her another drink when she spoke up again.

Willie, do you remember that night at the Dean when Mick asked me if I'd had any more MRIs?

Yes. I remember it well.

Well, I've got an appointment coming up. It's on Monday morning, actually. And I was wondering... well, I was wondering if I could ask you to come with me?

Willie didn't even have time to blink before he responded.

Of course. I'll swap shifts with Tiny. He can cover me during the day, and I'll go in later that night. So yeah, of course I'll come.

A limpidity came into her eyes, a look of absolute, untroubled serenity such that Willie had never seen before.

Thank you. Thank you.

The morning of the appointment, they decided to take a cab to the hospital, since the complexities of getting there via the rat's maze of subway lines was one stress they could easily do without. It dropped them off right in front of the Manhattan Cancer Center on the Upper East Side. Al's appointment was at the Breast Imaging Lab, which was located in a relatively new wing that was built at the foot of the larger, rectangular Research Building, which rose above it like some sort of giant, gleaming, silvery cell phone. They entered under a broad, concrete-and-brick awning, and wound their way through the pale hallways and robotic doors to the radiology check-in desk. Al gave her name and the name of her doctor, and in return the receptionist handed her a clipboard with several pages of forms to fill out. As they sat down in the faux-leather chairs to wait for her name to be called, Willie stole a glance at the first page of questions. What he saw looked quite literally comical:

HOW MUCH PAIN ARE YOU EXPERIENCING TODAY?
ZERO SIGNIFIES NO PAIN, TEN SIGNIFIES DEBILITATING PAIN.

☺+++++☺+++++☹

0 1 2 3 4 5 6 7 8 9 10

Are you serious? Smiley faces on your intake sheet?
I never really paid any attention to them.
Willie watched as she circled the number 6.
What do they give you for that?
Usually Lortab. But I don't always take them. They help with the pain, but not so much with the nausea and appetite thing.
Willie nodded, and picked up a two-month old copy of "Newsweek" to peruse silently while Al finished filling out her forms. When she completed them, she returned them to the check-in desk. This time, the receptionist handed her a pager.
When this goes off, a nurse will come through those doors over there and take you back.
Al nodded. She had been through this process many times before. When she returned to her seat, neither of them spoke for several minutes. Willie felt like a child, uncomfortable and awkward, as if it wasn't his place to speak unless spoken to. Al, on the other hand, was silent out of simple, unadulterated annoyance at having to be there in the first place. Eventually, though, she tossed out a morsel:
It's such a waste of a day, you know? I mean, it's one thing to go and lounge around in the park all day, but to spend hours in a hospital getting tested ... it feels like, I don't know, like atrophy.
Are you nervous or anxious at all?
No. I don't think it's possible for me to be nervous any more. It's just such a routine, and I've done it so many times now. Like, when I first moved into the neighborhood, I used to be kind of apprehensive about walking home late at night by myself. But now, it's just a fact of life. Something I have to do, you know?
Willie did know, and he nodded his head. But the hospital was a very new place to him, and he did feel very nervous and apprehensive, if only for her.

Al's pager flashed and vibrated, and she got up from her seat. Willie stood up too.

You can just hang out here. The MRI takes about forty-five minutes, and after that, my oncologist comes in to review the scans with me. There's a little coffee station over there with fruit and muffins and stuff if you get hungry. I'll be back in a couple of hours.

Okay. I'll see you then.

And good luck.

Al walked back into the lab accompanied by the attending nurse. Willie watched, standing, until the double doors swung shut behind them before sitting down again, and as he did so he couldn't help but wonder whether she felt like Napoleon entering Russia or like Sherman entering the South. He crossed and uncrossed his legs a number of times, like a nervous spider, unable to find a comfortable position. He scanned the circular room, examining the other waiting faces. Most of them were elderly, hairless, and completely devoid of any human feeling, emotions having long since been replaced by the stoicism of accepting the fact that a power, a force greater than that of their own will, had begun a slow yet consistent, concentrated war against their very own DNA, a deadly, undeviating confrontation whose violence and wreckage was in no way lessened by the microscopic battlefield upon which the forces of medical research and invention fought against the unnatural, uninhibited division of human cells. That was when Willie realized that this was a room teeming with pure desolation. *How long does one have to suffer this disease before they reach this point of acceptance? How long can one sustain the ability to deny? How long can they decline to accept the course of nature?*

Willie shook the thoughts from his head, and looked out again, surveying the waiting room anew. This time, he noticed a young, female face looking back at him. The woman behind it smiled warmly, got up from her chair, and walked across the room towards him. She was tall and slender, not skinny the way Al was, with long, straight, chocolate-brown hair.

Hi. I'm Jensen.

I'm Willie. It's nice to meet you.

I saw you two come in, and wanted to come over and introduce myself. This can be a pretty lonely place at times.

I'm learning that.

In a weird way, it sometimes reminds me of standing on a subway platform late at night. Mostly silent, mostly empty, and if there are any other people waiting there, they try not to make eye contact with each other.

Except for you.

I noticed you looking around first.

Jensen smiled again.

Anyway, like I said, I just wanted to say hello. She's lucky to have you. I wish I had a boyfriend who would come sit with me through all of this.

A boyfriend? Is that really what I look like to the world around us?

Um, yeah. I mean, of course. I don't really know what it's like for her to be going through this; I just try and be around, you know?

Yes. And she knows it too, so don't worry. What kind of cancer does she have?

Breast cancer.

Me too. I'm having radiation today. Five days a week, actually. This is round fifteen out of twenty. Here, look...

Jensen then grabbed a handful of her hair and pulled it over the top of her head. Willie was astonished to see it all come off in one continuous lock, revealing a shining white scalp underneath.

My hair already fell out.

I didn't even know that was a wig...

They're expensive, but they can make them pretty realistic these days. So what is your girlfriend here for today?

Uh, she's just having a regular MRI scan and checkup.

Oh, wow, I hate those things. Radiation takes like ten seconds, but sitting in those machines is so, I don't know, confining. I make them give me a Valium before I let them roll me in.

They talked for another few minutes until her pager buzzed. They both stood up. Jensen gave him a hug.

Maybe I'll see you two in here the next time you have an appointment!

I hope so. Good luck with the radiation.

Thanks!

Then she smiled again and exited through the same, swinging doors that had engulfed Al a short while before. Willie walked over to the snack cart and helped himself to a cup of coffee, a bagel, a plastic knife, and an individual tub of cream cheese. On his way back to his seat, he picked up a week-old copy of the *Village Voice*. Towards the back of the paper, the escort service ads featured pictures of girls flaunting their heavily bloated chests. Willie flipped it over and began reading from the front. He had read most of it and several other periodicals by the time Al emerged a few hours later.

Her face was ashen, and she strode quickly and decisively across the room. When the receptionist asked if she wanted to schedule her next appointment, she did not stop; she simply slowed down just enough to turn her head and say, *Call me*. Willie stood up, gathering their jackets from the waiting room chairs, but Al didn't so much as make eye contact as she walked on past him towards the exit. Willie followed her outside onto the street, hailed down a cab, and opened the door for Al before climbing in himself. They were twenty blocks away before he mustered the courage to ask,

What did they say?

Still silent, Al reached into her pocket and pulled out a twice-folded piece of paper, which she handed to Willie. He opened it up. It was a computer print-out containing a page of text that was written in the esoteric, strange, and almost foreign language of the medical profession. Willie slowly read over each and every word of the print-out with the slightly delusional belief (or was it hope?) that he might be able to understand it in the end by some emergent property of language itself:

> TECHNIQUE: Multiplanar, multisequence imaging of the chest was performed pre- and post-contrast with IV administration of 20 cc of gadolinium.
>
> FINDINGS: There is a multiloculated heterogeneous mass with nonenhancing cystic and enhancing solid components within the left lymphatic node abutting the atrium of the left lateral ventricle. There is significant confluent surrounding white matter T2 hyperintensity with associated sulcal effacement representing edema. The largest enhancing portion of the mass measures approximately 3.4 x 2.0 cm in maximal axial dimension. There is a nonenhancing multiseptated cystic component just superior measuring approximately 2.8 x 2.3 cm in maximal axial diameter. The greatest extent of the entire mass measures approximately 3.9 cm.
>
> IMPRESSION: Multiseptated heterogeneous left lymphatic node mass with nonenhancing cystic and enhancing solid components with surrounding edema and mass effect without associated restricted diffusion. This lesion is most consistent with metastatic tumor.

Al, I don't understand... what does this mean?

The last two words are the only ones you need to know.

It's come back...

Just get me home. Just get me the fuck home.

The cab ride from the hospital back to Brooklyn was a very long and a very quiet one. By the time they finally arrived back at their building, the sun was nearing the end of its descent, and long shadows were beginning to reach out across the street like clutching, covetous fingers. Al opened the cab door and went swiftly from the car to the building entrance, dug her keys out of her purse, and entered the foyer; Willie was in such a rush to catch up that he paid the driver double the fair without even realizing it. When he got inside himself, he found Al standing at the end of the long, ground floor hallway in front of her door, not moving, not speaking, not even turning to look at him. Willie walked slowly up behind her and put his hand on her shoulder.

Hey, you want me to come in? Hang out for a while?

No, I know you gotta get to the diner.

Forget about it. I'll take a sick day. Tiny knows I was going to the hospital today, but I never told him why.

No, just go take care of your shift. I'll be okay. I promise. I knew this was going to have to deal with this sooner or later. It happens, you know? It just fucking happens. I just want to lie down and—I don't know—just let it all sink in. Just marinade a bit. Okay?

You promise you'll be alright?

I promise.

Okay then. But call if you need anything. I can't always hear my cell phone when I'm in the kitchen, but you can always call the diner and have Gus come find me.

I'll be fine. Just get going before you're late. I didn't think the appointment was going to take so long today, but thank you for coming.

Thank you for letting me come.

Willie offered what he thought might be a hopeful smile. Al offered a muted grin in return, and then they each entered their own apartments.

When the door closed behind him, Willie felt somehow rudderless, adrift in his own home. His shift started in just over half an hour, but going in and working that night seemed very wrong. *I should just call in sick. It's not going to be a busy night. Not even for dinner. Tiny will stay on for a second shift. He'll probably even appreciate the extra hours. I should just hang here for an hour or so and then go over and check on her. But... maybe she really just wants to be alone for awhile. I mean, she did say she'd be okay. She even promised. You should trust her, man. Just trust her. She's been through this before, and you haven't. You wouldn't get it. You wouldn't even know what to say.*

And with that, Willie changed into his checkered chef pants and got ready to leave. When he arrived at the diner, he said hello to Gus and went into the back to punch his time card and sharpen his knives. As he had expected, the early traffic was slow. There was more noise coming out of the kitchen than there was chatter in the dining room. And it stayed like that for two or three hours. That is, until he got an order ticket for a hot pastrami on rye with slaw on the side. He stacked the meat high on the bread, took the plate over to the ceramic counter, and was just about to slide it under the heat lamps for the server to come pick it up when he overheard two morbidly obese women with Southern accents yammering away at a nearby table.

Did you see that checkout boy at the bookstore today?

The tall skinny one with the crew cut and glasses?

Yes, that was him. Do you know who he reminded me of?

Who's that?

It's... oh, what's his name, the actor on ER. You know... the one they killed off with the brain tumor?

Willie had to grit his teeth to keep from calling them out. *You ignorant fucking wretch. You're a diabetic fucking heart attack time bomb waiting to go off, and you talk about people's health problems like that?* When he returned to the kitchen, there was a look of patent disgust on his face. Tiny cocked an eyebrow and asked him,

You look like a fucking blivet, man. What's up?

Just the shit that some people say.

Fuck that shit, man.

Fuck that shit.

He was about to let it go at that when the kitchen doors swung open, and Bella, the server, came in carrying the plate he had just laid out for the customer. The look on Willie's face went from one of disgust to sheer, unadulterated incredulity.

You've gotta be fucking kidding me...

She says she ordered a side of potato salad...

She ordered the fucking cole slaw...

I know she did, that's why I wrote it on the ticket. But she's all huffed up now about her potato salad, and...

Willie cut her off in mid-sentence with the point of a finger. He strode over to the stack of tickets impaled on the spindle near the register, grabbed a fistful, and made his way directly over to the table where the two obnoxiously capacious women were sitting, and accosted them.

What's the fucking problem? Your country fried steak ass brain couldn't remember your goddamn order or what? Here, take a fucking look...

And with that, Willie flung the wad of tickets directly in the women's faces. Then, he spun around on his heels, and walked directly out the front door of the diner, in plain view of the other customers, some of whom were astonished, some snickering, with one table in all out applause. *I'm outta here, baby. Outta here like last year. I am fucking gone.*

He was still muttering to himself when he arrived back at his building. When he reached the end of the long, faux-terrazzo hallway and found himself standing in front of Al's apartment door, he heard loud, brash music thundering from within. He knocked once with his knuckles, and then a second time, some seconds later, pounding away with the heel of his hand. Finally, he heard something: first the nightlatch and then the deadbolt disengaged, and finally the door swung open. Al stood there, looking more pensive than plaintive. *She looks introspective, really. Analytic. Maybe even philosophical. But she hasn't been crying. I can see that much in her eyes.* Then she took a step back in a silent invitation to enter.

Willie walked in wordlessly and sat down on the couch, and Al turned down the music, though she didn't quite turn it off. Then she settled into a big roundabout chair on the opposite wall, facing Willie. They both became quite still and silent, almost afraid to move, and instead of making eye contact, each of them looked around at the various mundane elements that surrounded them each and every day, existing on the periphery of their vision, and which somehow were never before worth so much as a glance: wall sockets, baseboards, door jambs, et cetera. A sense of peace settled over them like dust, blanketing the room, even the immaterial music itself, and Willie felt, with a sort of bemused amazement, like he had just leapt into a pool of water without leaving so much as a ripple. And it was exactly because of that feeling that he hesitated as long as he did before breaking the surface of that sense of peace with what he had been wanting to ask her all day.

Have you talked to anybody in your family about it yet?

Al shook her head.

I haven't spoken to them in a long time.

Why? What happened?

My brother disappeared.

You mean he was kidnapped?

No. He just left. Vanished. Se fue. And my parents blame me.

How come?

It's a long story, but basically it all started when his fiancée left him. I really liked her, too. She was fucking cool. But after that, he just broke apart. Couldn't take it anymore. Everything around him seemed to remind him of her.

I know how that goes.

But with him, he never came around. I mean, he never snapped out of it. He just got deeper and deeper, got more and more depressed. I think it was the first time in his life that he ever felt hate. Everything there at home reminded him of her, and so he began to hate all of it. And that's why he did it. At least, that's why I think he did.

Did what?

He embezzled money from the greenhouse. He basically stole from his own family. From us. Took out thousands of dollars in traveler's checks, and then he just took off. He told everybody that he was going to a horticultural conference at Penn State. Everyone except for me.

He told you he was leaving?

Yes. I even remember what he said.

What was that?

He said, "If you want to be erased, you have to do it to yourself." After that, nobody ever heard from him again.

I don't really know what to say.

Anyway, I ended up telling my parents that he confided in me, and, well, now they're not talking to me either. I guess maybe they thought they could have stopped him if I told them. I don't know. The point is—to answer your question—I lost a sister-in-law, a brother, and both my parents. I didn't even talk to them when I was first diagnosed.

I can't believe you took all that on by yourself...

Me neither. And you know what? Before I did, I asked myself the exact same question that you just asked me tonight.

Really?

Yes. I asked it of myself every which way I could think of. I read *You Can't Go Home Again,* the whole fucking thing, and when I got to the end, I thought to myself, Maybe Thomas Wolfe was right. I mean, he even died before it was ever published, right? He didn't live long enough to see his own book to find a home on a shelf somewhere. But then Robert Fagles translated *The Odyssey*, and I read that too. I thought, maybe it just takes a mythical, maybe even a supra-human figure to endure the ten slow, painful years that it takes to struggle home. So I decided that if the King of Ithaca could find his way home, then I could do that too. I made him my pattern, my symbol. My guide, even. The only thing is, I haven't quite arrived yet.

They both fell silent again after that, leaving only the low music in the background to occupy the space of the apartment. Willie was unsure whether to speak or keep quiet, but the passage of time began to bother him. *Sixty seconds becomes a long time when nothing at all is happening. And the second sixty is even longer still. If I keep this up, eventually the clock on the wall is going to grind to a halt.* So he decided on the former.

What do you feel like doing?

You know, it's strange. It's strange, but it's not about what I feel like doing. It's simply about what I feel. The first time it happened, I refused to believe it. At least, that's what I felt right after my diagnosis. But then my oncologist and my radiologist and my surgeon laid out this course of action, and everything was so specific... too detailed and specific to deny any more. And everyone talks about it in terms of fighting, you know? "You're tough, you're a fighter, you'll beat this," they say. So I started looking at cancer as my enemy, my foe, something to battle, mentally as well as physically. Even militarily, I guess. So when treatment was over, I felt as if I'd been honorably discharged from the service, like I was now a veteran of the International Armed Forces of Mischance and Bad Fucking Luck.

That must have been a relief...

Well, it was, but maybe not the way you're thinking it was. You see, after all that, I realized that, in the end, it was never a question of 'if,' but rather of 'when.' I knew that the little rebel cancer cells would rise up again. It's really just a proletarian disease if you think about it. And a stubborn motherfucker, too. They can cut out as much tumor as they want, they can bomb away at the surgical bed with all the radiation of Hiroshima, Nagasaki, and Chernobyl combined, and they can poison whatever is left with some Agent Orange chemotherapy. But if you take a tiny piece of flesh out and put it under the microscope, you'll see cancer cells there, hiding in the walls like roaches. Consistent, constant, and steady. That's all remission really is, and there is a sense of peace that comes with that acceptance. The roaches will sit there, biding their time, focusing their undeviated menace for years, and then—with all of mother nature's tragic sense of violence and catastrophe to draw on, and in spite of her universal imagination, her gift for artistry and design—they come lunging back. Lightning will strike twice, and the floodwaters will rise again. The first one is always a surprise, but the resurgence is inevitable. Vindictive, too.

At that point, Al fell silent, and Willie had understood enough to know not to interrupt it this time, for she was continuing the same process of understanding and acceptance which she'd begun hours earlier, before he'd ever arrived. *Well, it's happened now, and there's only one direction to go from here. Just when the flood was beginning to recede and reveal the surface of the ground again, the surge of water came back. It's more like the tide, really, than a flood. A riptide, an undertow. But either way, it's a part of my past, and it's a part of my life, too. Maybe even part of my legacy. Willie was right, though, to ask about my family. He might honestly be the closest thing to that which I've got left. Three years ago, when it happened the first time, my husband blamed me. I left him, even though I knew that doing so would leave me completely alone. So I might not have a family anymore, but since that night when Willie knocked on my door, I've been having fun exploring the neighborhood and everything, and slowly, gradually, it's starting to feel like I've found a home. As much, even, as it was like growing up in Cartago, Colombia, way back when. As if old Carthage herself were being reborn in the New World. I wonder if he'd like to go back with me and visit... go back and walk along the banks of the Río de la Vieja, so brown he'd probably think it was filled with cocoa powder, watch it slide placidly towards the Atlantic Ocean, past the banks where the cattle drink and spanned by a rich green looming, chuppah-like canopy of ceiba trees. The earth is poor there, but grandpa used the greenhouse to create such rich soil that the flowers he grew almost didn't need to be planted. You could almost just hold a chrysanthemum seed up to it and it would take and grow. He would plant in the early Spring, and by the end of May the greenhouse would be filled with symmetric rows of strong, six-inch stalks; by August they were a full three feet tall, well-branched and in full bloom. The greenhouse was an epidemic of color—pure white, yellow, bronze, pink and lavender, coral and salmon, purple, and deep burgundy red—the air was sweet, warmed by the lamplight and humidified by the brief yet frequent misting. There was a store just a short way down the river where the farmers would come with their sleepy, rope-bridled burros to buy tobacco and mosquito netting. The vigilante was usually there too, along with his dog. I remember that goddamn dog; it was the only dog I'd ever seen with blue eyes, and it was the only thing I liked about that little podunk country town. All I wanted to do then was go to the all night parties at the salsatecas in downtown Cali, dance to techno and house music, drink refajo and aguardiente until the sun came up, have a breakfast of arepas and coffee, and eventually go to sleep. But I don't want to dance any-more. I just want to go back to the greenhouse and walk up and down the rows. Maybe even with Willie holding my hand...*

At long last, she spoke again, though without looking at him.

Sometimes, I feel like I've never been more alone in my life. But I just wanted to say that I'm really glad you're here. That we met.

I'm glad too. I know exactly what you mean.

Then Al reached for her bowl which was resting there on the coffee table. She pulled out a cigarette lighter and sparked it, put the pipe to her lips, touched the flame to the weed, and inhaled. She held the lung-ful of smoke for a couple of long seconds before releasing it up into the revolving blades of the ceiling fan.

You know, the first time around, when I was going through chemo and the divorce and all, I felt so bad in every conceivable way that I would wake up every morning, look out the window, and ask myself whether that day would be a good day to die. So far, that answer has been no.

I can't even imagine what it must have been like to have all of that going on around you at once.

It wasn't fun. That's for damn sure. You know how people will say that they wouldn't wish something on their worst enemy? Well I used to tell myself that I'd most definitely wish cancer on my worst enemy. Why? Because it usually ends up killing them. But there was a problem with that kind of reasoning.

What was that?

My own worst enemy was the cancer itself. So I let that go, and kept on looking for something else, something more decent, more honorable, something that didn't end with revenge. After what I've been through, I'll never feel like that again. I'll never be that afraid. Not of death, not of anything. They say that hell is the absence of God. But I'll tell you this... I don't know if I believe in God, but I do know that peace is the absence of fear. I learned that the hard way, but I think I learned it the best way, too.

You learned how to accept...

Yes, that's it, exactly. Acceptance. Hey, you're kind of a nerdy, bookish guy, right? Look at this...

Al returned her bowl to its place on the coffee table, stood up, and went to the bookcase. She selected a lean paperback and leafed through the pages before dogearing one and passing it to Willie to read. Willie accepted the slim volume, and looked at the page. It had been worn thin from frequent perusal, and one particular paragraph had been carefully underlined in blue ink:

> Meditation on inevitable death should be performed daily. Every day when one's body and mind are at peace, one should meditate upon being ripped apart by arrows, rifles, spears and swords, being carried away by surging waves, being thrown into the midst of a great fire, being struck by lightning, being shaken to death by a great earthquake, falling from thousand-foot cliffs, dying of disease or committing seppuku at the death of one's master. And every day without fail one should consider himself as dead. There is a saying of the elders' that goes, "Step from under the eaves and you're a dead man. Leave the gate and the enemy is waiting." This is not a matter of being careful. It is to consider oneself as dead beforehand. When you are resolved from the beginning, you will not suffer. This understanding extends to all.

Al took another hit from her bowl while Willie read the page. When he had finished, he flipped the book over to examine the cover: *Hagakure: The Book of the Samurai* by Yamamoto Tsunetomo, it read. Translated by William Scott Wilson. He handed it back to Al before speaking.

Peace and understanding lead to acceptance. I like it.

And then, silently, to himself: *And I wish I had read it a long time ago. It took a prison term for me to learn what I could have gotten out of this thin little book.*

Willie rubbed his eyes and abruptly changed the subject.

Hey, what were you listening to when I knocked on the door? I didn't mean to interrupt... you can turn it back up if you want to.

Actually, I was doing just what the book says. A little meditation, set to music. Here, think about this...

Al grabbed the remote and cycled the CDs around for a moment before she found the track that she wanted. Willie recognized it instantly.

Metallica. *Creeping Death.* You can mediate to this?

Oh yeah. That's what's so great about this song. See, everybody thinks it's just some cold-ass Jules Winnfield shit, you know? But what it's really about is an affirmation of life. I mean, sure, it's all about the final plague in Exodus and the killing of the firstborn, but it's told from the archangel's point of view. So the only people dying are the slave masters. You know, "lamb's blood on the door... I shall pass." And the Israelites are freed. I listened to it all the time when I was first diagnosed, wondering whether I would be chosen as one of the people cancer would pass over.

And you were...

I was. Once. But like I said, the healthier I got, the more I began to understand the fact that it wasn't a question of if it would come back, it was a question of when. It took me a long time, but like I said, I found a way to accept it, to come to terms with it. The Hagakure helped me a lot with that early on. And then, when this came out...

She picked up the remote again and selected a new disc.

... I knew I was at peace with the other extreme.

Willie knew this song too. It was *Like a Stone* by Audioslave. Al's eyes were reddened now, and she was very much enjoying this chance to relate her personal philosophies to someone other than herself. This was all quite clear to Willie, who was completely captivated by this thoughtful young woman. *She's pensive without being brooding, reflective and introspective without seeming wistful or self-absorbed. And the sound of her voice is beautiful...*

How did you know?

Well, the first time I heard it I thought it was sort of a sad love song, you know, what my grandpa used to call an hado, about a guy waiting to see whether the woman he loved would ever come back to him or some shit like that. But when I really listened to the lyrics, I realized it was all about an old man reminiscing over all his friends and family who have already passed away. So he's sitting there in this hotel room, reading the Bible, and wondering if he'll be allowed into Paradise, because he's not a religious man. So he's just sitting there, waiting to find out whether or not he'll ever see them again.

You know, it's like you're putting together a soundtrack to your own funeral or something...

No sooner had he blurted that out than did Willie hate himself for having done so. He immediately began stammering out an apology.

Ah, fuck me... I'm sorry... I don't know what the hell I was thinking. I didn't mean to go there...

No, it's okay, really. You're actually kind of right. Some things don't mean quite what they used to mean to me.

Willie exhaled a mental sigh of relief. He couldn't believe what he'd said, but he also couldn't believe how interested, how involved he was, or how open and honest Al seemed to be. He decided to press on, at least a bit:

Do you ever wonder about that? I mean, wonder about what might happen when...

Willie couldn't bring himself to complete the question. But Al picked up the threads of his thought like a baton from a relay runner.

Oh, for sure. I mean, it's something I ask myself all the time. But the way I see it, I'm not worried about what will become of my own life. I know what the future holds. Ultimately, I mean. We all do. So I choose to focus on what I've left behind. Whether I've done anything with a sense of permanence to it. And I'm just not sure that I've been able to do that yet.

Willie felt his pulse begin to quicken. *She's been the biggest single thing in my whole entire life since I ended up here in this neighborhood. Since I restarted my life, actually. I wonder if she knows that, or if she even thinks about it. But what I'm afraid to do is wonder whether I might come to mean anything to her, anything of significance, anything of permanence...*

Something tells me that you already have, even if you don't know about it yet.

Al tried to laugh it off with a bit of awkward sarcasm, though inwardly she was much obliged. When she collected herself a moment later, she spoke:

I do know one thing, though.

What's that?

I know I'm not going to just bow out gracefully and exit stage left. I'm gonna go down swinging!

What do you mean, like Sonny Liston?

She laughed again, this time more comfortably.

No, like Benny Goodman!

Willie grinned.

Not like Papa Hem though, right?

Of course not.

What about Dylan Thomas?

Not like him either. I mean, the guy could write about rage and the dying of the light and all, but somehow he couldn't do it in his own damn life.

How about Sammy Davis?

Yeah. Or a Tommy Dorsey.

How about Charlie Mingus?

And Bob Marley, of course!

Al was beaming back at him. She was enjoying this macabre little brainstorming session, but she was enjoying even more the simple fact that Willie was enjoying it too. As they enjoyed that moment of shared laughter together, Willie was reminded that, some years earlier, he had read somewhere that Doc Holliday's legendary fearlessness didn't come from carrying a gun or even from being unbeatably quick on the draw; rather, it was from the knowledge that he had already been condemned to death by tuberculosis, and therefore was simply unconcerned with any threat that might be posed by whistling bullets. *There are some things of which the dying know more than the dead...*

Seriously though. Tell me this, if you're really wondering about leaving a mark and that sort of thing, why don't you look into publishing some of that poetry you were telling me about? You know, on your grandfather's old typewriter? I mean it...

Al rolled her eyes.

God, I don't know. I don't know the first thing about the publishing business. It's not like I have an MFA; hell, I never even took a writing class.

Who cares? I thought that poem you read for me was William Carlos Williams, remember? But it was you. Your experience, your words. People would read them.

This time, Al laughed without any added sarcasm.

Now you're starting to sound like the old ghost from "Field of Dreams!" Besides, all poetry is missing something.

What's that?

Music!

Al's eyes were still bloodshot, but there was an undeniably gleeful sheen in them as well, and they were alight with that joy as she continued to speak.

Here, there's one more song I want to play for you. It's by my old friend, Ludwig Van, full of bliss and heaven!

Many years later, wherever and whenever he would hear it, Willie was to remember that night, for it was the first time he had ever heard Opus 125, the Symphony No. 9 in D minor. It opened up in a torrent, a tumultuous rush that transpired into a strong, clear, driving theme, as if a feral horse were being broken and bridled for the first time. He listened as it galloped on, spurred to speed by tympani and trombones, until variations in the theme emerged: buoyant, nimble horns, brisk, energetic, alert trumpets, and frolicsome, high-spirited violins. But the choral finale is what shook him the most. Willie felt completely disarmed and thoroughly enlivened. He spoke not one word of German, but he knew what Elysium was, and that even deaf men can smell fields of asphodel. When it finally concluded in a burst of beautiful, prancing sparks of joy, Al looked to Willie for a reaction. She was beaming.

I've never heard anything like it.

I think it's the most complete work of art ever made.

How come?

Because its creativity involves so many people. Beethoven composed the music, Schiller wrote the poetry, the orchestra plays its instruments, and the vocalists sing the lyrics. It includes everything, mind and body alike. It's got the stuff of both strength and courage in it, and that makes it greater than any novel, any painting, any song, or any sculpture. It's both heart and soul, bone and blood, painful flesh and surpassing spirits. That's why I think it's so full, so complete.

Al picked up her bowl and tried to take one final hit, but it was cashed out. Willie watched the subtle movements of her body, from the lithe reach of her arm as she placed the pipe back on the coffee table to the quick flash of her eyelashes blinking. He was still watching her when her eyes turned back to meet his.

Come sit with me.

Al slowly eased herself up and out of the big roundabout chair. Willie continued to watch as she made her way across the tiny, smoke-filled room, and as she did so, time seemed to wind itself down to the point where everything began to take place in a slow-motion version of reality. Even the leisurely turning blades of the ceiling fan appeared to slow down, as if they had been somehow transformed into the second hand of an old pocket watch. Al sat down on the couch next to him and drew her knees up onto the cushion, and Willie gently wrapped his arm around her shoulders. As he did so, Al hummed softly.

Thank you.

For what?

For coming with me. For helping me out. For everything.

You shouldn't thank me for that. I was just trying to do the right thing. I mean, what else could I have done?

Al ignored the question.

You're just so amazing. All things considered.

What do you mean, all things considered?

Exactly what I said. All things considered.

Willie gave her a little squeeze with his arm. He felt excited and peaceful all at the same time. He understood her, felt the light of truth in her, and that was something he hadn't known in a long, long time. A minute later, Al was sleeping peacefully on his shoulder, and a few minutes after that, Willie was sleeping peacefully too, both with her and with the knowledge she had proffered. They slept there, together on the couch, until a belligerent pounding on the door woke them early in the morning.

Still groggy, Al got to her feet and was making her way to the door when she heard a voice from the hallway call out,

NYPD... WE NEED TO ASK YOU A FEW QUESTIONS...

I'm coming!

Then, as she pretended to fumble with the latches, she turned to Willie and hissed, hide the bowl!

Willie grabbed it off the coffee table and jammed it into the pocket of his chef pants, which he was still wearing, just in time before Al opened the door, revealing the two officers standing there.

Sorry to disturb you so early, ma'am, but we just need to ask you a few questions about your neighbor next door...

It was then that the two officers saw Willie standing there in the background. Willie recognized them both immediately as officers Scagnetti and Coffey.

Ah, so that's why you didn't answer your door this morning. Why don't you step out into the hallway here. We got a call last night about an incident at the diner up on Washington, and we need you to answer some questions.

No. This cannot be happening. Not now. Please. Not now...

Willie stepped out into the hallway with Officer Coffey, while Officer Scagnetti remained inside to talk to Al.

I gotta tell you, blowing up and walking out on a job that a police officer got you was a very, very bad decision on your part.

I guess it was. *No no no... Not after everything that happened in the last twenty-four hours...*

I gotta tell you this, too: after what happened last night at the diner, I've got cause for a search.

There's no way you got a warrant that fast...

I didn't. And I don't need one. It's all under the terms of your probation agreement. And since I found you in someone else's apartment, I need to confirm you're living at the address listed in your file.

It's been awhile since you guys came by for a visit. *Not again... Not after everything that has happened in the past year...*

So do want to open the door for me?

What happens if I say no?

Pretty much the same thing as if you say yes.

Willie reached for his pocket, where his keys were stowed, but Officer Coffey barked sharply at him. He had moved his right hand to the holster hanging from his belt.

Hold it! Keep your hands where I can see them. You've got your keys in your pocket there?

Yes sir.

Do you have anything else on you that might hurt me? Any needles or knives or anything like that?

No sir.

All right then...

Officer Coffey reached into Willie's pockets and withdrew his money clip, his cell phone, his keys, and... the bowl.

Well well well... What do we have here? This just might be a violation... unless there's anything you want to tell me about?

Willie felt completely undone, felt the twin hopes of love and freedom rush out of his body like blood from a butchered hog strung up in a packing plant, and therefore had no fight left in his eyes when he looked up at Officer Coffey and answered.

Nothing I don't want to tell a lawyer first.

Have it your way. I'm placing you under arrest for possession of drug paraphernalia and for violating the conditions of your parole…

The next thing that Willie heard was the Christmassy jingle bell sound of Officer Coffey taking out his handcuffs. ◆

The Valley

MO SWUNG HIS CAR onto West 178th Street. A few turns and merges later, he was on the lower level of the George Washington Bridge heading towards Fort Lee, New Jersey. In the center lane of West bound traffic, he found himself surrounded on all sides by steel I-beams and rivets, as if he were rushing headlong down a cell block in a mile-long prison. The day was terribly hot, but everything about this structure felt cold, fierce, and precise. Mo, on the other hand, was feeling haggard and leaden, as if he were still hung over from his failed attempt at what he thought was love, still trying to sleep off the last few remnants of that dark, illicit passion instead of reconciling himself with the fact that he'd gotten exactly what he paid for. Peace and happiness and all the glorious possibilities they bring to life hadn't passed him by; in fact, they weren't even on the same road as him. Mo turned off the A/C and opened his window, but the humming of his tires on the asphalt and the thrashing of his hair in the wind did little to clear his mind. *The last time I drove across water, I was heading up to Lake George. With her. Now, I'm heading to Jersey... with this.* He glanced at his jacket on the passenger seat. *What the hell am I doing? There are limits to these things, limits to sin, to deceit, to how far you can go underground. But now I know that there are limits to how far a person can go in the opposite direction, too: limitations on love, on trust, on honesty, and on the truth. There is no* *exit in either direction, no escape. There is only the road.*

He was past the second anchorage now, and as he bore left onto the Jersey Turnpike, heading South, the monotonous drone of his tires took on a softer tone, though he still squinted furiously into the steady rush of wind in his face. In the offing lay the Meadowlands. *A grand euphemism if ever there was one. The Marshlands would be more appropriate. South Jersey has the barren pine heaths, and North Jersey is a fucking marsh. Nothing but mud flats and giant cattails and the sour smell of rotting mussels. You wouldn't bury Jimmy Hoffa in a meadow. Not like the one in the North Woods, anyway.* It was then that Mo felt the distinct impression that he was leaving home on a trip of some duration, rather than just for the afternoon. He thought about his building back on 108th Street, thought about the front stoop leading up to the heavy outer door, and he stopped himself right there. *You don't want to run back inside. Don't need to, don't have to either. It's all behind me now, just like the bridge, just like the past.* Mo rolled his window almost to the top, leaving just a fraction of an inch open through which the sibilant wind continued to rush. He turned on the radio and scanned through the stations; Roy Orbison was singing about lonely people lost in love. Mo kept scanning until he hit 97.1.

He was seeing signs for Secaucus now. *I wonder if I should have just ended it like that. If I just threw it all away when the shit got deep. What was it I said? You treacherous fucking bitch. That was it. Damn. It's always easier to fight your way out than to negotiate, to wait, to think. Maybe I should have been a little more steady, a little more careful. She came to me once, right? I mean, she might have come back around again, and if she did, she might have been able to find a foothold, to find something to hang on to. I might have fucked up the best part of my life by trying to throw out the trash. I could still get off at Exit 17 and go back to New York through the Lincoln Tunnel. I could still turn around...* He began nervously checking his mirrors and blind spots, and his breathing grew quick and shallow. And he could not stop it, could not stop the panic though he could feel it, acute and sudden, hitting him as inevitably and physically as the wind, his breath growing thinner and thinner, barely touching his lungs before rushing out, fleeing, leaving a vacuum behind, an emptiness that could only be filled with the twin pangs of guilt and regret. *She might want to turn back too. Yes, I think so. She would come back. Eventually. There would be a buzz at the door one day and it would be her. I would let her in, and she wouldn't even bother with the elevator; she'd take the stairs, sprint up them, two at a time, and I'd be there at the landing, waiting for her, listening to the urgency of her steps, and when she finally reached it, breathless, she would have collapsed, sobbing, into my arms, and all I would be able to say was It's okay, baby, you're back now, you're back, and everything's going to be all right now, everything's going to be all right. It would be as if no departure had ever taken place, no treachery committed, no ugly ugly words spoken… everything would be everything, and it would be as it should be.*

The driver of an SUV slammed on his horn. Mo had drifted out of his lane of traffic. *Don't be a fucking fool. She's the one who fucked everything up. I'm just the one who's letting go. She can hold on to herself now. It's as simple as that. It wouldn't even have mattered if you never said what you did. Saying nothing would have been even worse. Silence is uncaring, silence is disdain, silence is malignant. Hatred, at least, has passion underneath it.* The Kearny exit was coming up on the right, and the Pulaski Skyway lay to his left, which meant more cantilevers, more trusses, more prison-like steel. Through his hissing window he could see the local streets and the New Jersey Transit railroad network before they gave way to the lethargic Hackensack River, laden with silt and scummed with floating garbage. Industrial shipping crates were stacked as high as a four-story building on both sides of the road. He wished he had brought something with him, wished that he had stopped at a bodega before leaving for a Jamaican beef patty or even a bottle of Coke… anything to calm his stomach down. *That's it. You just have to calm down. Stay cool, don't wig out, and you get the job done. You get it done and tonight you'll be back at the Lion's Den, back with the regulars, back with the people who work or hustle their way though the most sunlit days so they can eat, drink, and be merry that night without ever having to waist a single thought about their fate. Yes. That is what it will be now, for me.*

He was past Jersey City now, and he could see the Anheuser-Bush brewery and Newark Liberty Airport up ahead. Mo was feeling more relaxed now, ready to settle down for the rest of the drive. It should be easy enough, for he could rattle off turnpike exits as if they were letters of the alphabet. It would be more boring than anything else. The radio had switched over to a talk show program, and he hit the scan button again, trying to find something with music. As he waited for a station to pop up, he had the vague realization that there was nothing even remotely Garden about this State. Not this part of it, anyway. Every square inch that wasn't paved over to form a road had been taken over by radio relay towers, high-tension wires, rugged, decrepit factories and refineries that glowed in the night with a dirty, unnatural radiance. Coming up ahead was the city of Elizabeth, with its impoverished industrial backyard, and beyond that lay the hulking prison, where the sinners may pass from Rahway to Yahweh. It wasn't visible from the turnpike, but Mo knew it because a few kids from the old neighborhood ended up serving time there for crimes they committed in Jersey. That, and the fact that the prison's massive, central dome looked disturbingly like the dome atop the library-turned-administrative building back at the University.

He was starting to see signs for New Brunswick now, and he checked his mirrors again, looking for a chance to ease over into the exit lane. A few cars ahead of him, someone in a black Escalade was attempting to do the same thing, and narrowly missed sideswiping a driver in a 1970's Dodge Charger. As they exchanged angry horn blasts, Mo applied a little pressure the brake. He did not want to miss the connection to US-1, which would take him the rest of the way to Princeton Junction, since there would be nothing fashionable about being late. Not for this appointment. Exit 9 was coming up just ahead. Mo left the turnpike and merged onto US-1 South towards Trenton. For about fifteen miles traffic continued moving, smooth and uneventful. He was past New Brunswick now, about to hit Lawrenceville. And there, almost immediately, he found himself ensnared in a sea of idling vehicles. In this sea, however, the sounds of the gulls were replaced by car horns, and instead of the salty air, the smells of exhaust and burnt oil were wafting in through his window. *But you're fine. Don't push it. You'll get there right on time. Then it's just do the deed and it's over man, it's over. You can do whatever you want after that. Even go into town, chill out, get a goddamn hoagie, and take a look at that other ivy-laced school there. See what that place is like. Or you can just get the fuck outta dodge, head back to the city, hook up with King, and lose yourself at the fucking Den for the night. After that, it's a brand new day. And all you gotta do is be cool and do the deed. Be cool and do the goddamn deed.*

He nervously checked his cell phone. King hadn't called to check on him yet, which was about as reassuring as it was nerve-wracking. He looked out though the windshield: as far as he could see in front of him, there was no construction, no accidents, no red lights, nothing to clue him in as to the cause of the jam-up. He was caught in the middle of three lanes of motionless traffic; flanking the lane to his left was the concrete barrier separating the southbound traffic from the northbound. To his right was the merging lane, which had also filled up with cars. For five minutes, nobody moved more than a couple of feet. Then some movement opened up in the left-hand lane. Mo clicked on his turn signal and made his way over as soon as a generous driver let him with a nod and a wave. *There must be a jam-up on the merging lane. The next intersection is just a mile or two ahead. Once I get past that, I should be in the clear.* But after passing seven or eight cars, his lane once again ground to a standstill. For another five or six minutes, he sat there in silence. There was no longer any breeze filtering in through his window, so he rolled it up, turned the A/C back on, and waited for another five minutes until traffic in the middle lane began to move. But by the time he had made his way back to the lane in which he had started, the movement had inevitably come to a halt. Mo checked his cell phone again, and then double-checked the time on the clock on the dashboard. *Somebody better start moving soon. Because this isn't looking too good.* He was getting jittery now, and he tried to still his nerves by gripping the steering wheel more tightly, the way he had gripped a handgun once when his hand began to tremble in anticipation of squeezing the trigger. Five more minutes. This time, the lane to his right began to open up a bit. He threw on his blinker, took a hard breath, exhaled, and waited for someone to let him merge in front of them. The first few cars simply ignored him as they eased by, but as they did so, Mo noticed that the merging lane was now largely free of traffic. *If I can make it over there, I can just drive up the road a piece and then cut back into traffic before the next light.* And then, he got his chance. A car slowed down behind him, and Mo spun the wheel, passing through the right lane of traffic before settling into the merging lane on the far right edge of the road. Maybe a hundred yards down the road in front of him was the sign for the Washington Road exit into Princeton. He checked the dashboard clock one more time, just to be sure. And that was when he noticed the lights flashing in his rear view mirror.

Mo slowed down reflexively, on the off chance that the officer was going to pass him in pursuit of some other character. But no, the car closed on him quickly, decisively, its siren silent, its lights blaring like strobes in a nightclub. It was the lights that gave the car the illusion of magic in an all too real world, as if it had suddenly materialized out of the thick, midday air and landed directly behind him in traffic, when it fact it had simply been laying in the cut, waiting for someone to provoke it, providing the magic with reason enough to show its true self. His speed reduced to a mere crawl, Mo made the right turn off the highway and onto Washington Road, even taking care to signal before pulling onto the shoulder a few yards later, and turned off the ignition. The patrol car stopped a few lengths behind him and sat there, lights still flashing angrily, furious even, as if calling attention to its quarry's transgression. Through his mirror, Mo could see that it was a Ford Crown Victoria—*How the fuck could I have driven past a Crown Vic without noticing it?*—and could read the state license plate through the grill guards on the front bumper just as surely as the officer behind the wheel was reading his own tags at that same moment. After a minute or two, the officer exited his vehicle and began to walk in a slow, deliberate manner towards Mo's window. Mo couldn't see his face in the side mirror, but he could clearly make out was the patently obvious clip-on tie and the yellow-striped pants of the New Jersey State Police. He opened his window; there was no breeze here, just the rasping sound of the officer's stiff shoes on the loose roadside gravel.

Good afternoon, I'm Officer Cerreta. I'll need to take a look at your driver's license and vehicle registration.

Those things I've got. What I don't have is a clean conscience.

Yes sir. I've got my license right here...

He dug his money clip out of his left front pocket, pulled out the citrus-colored New York State driver license, and handed it over.

The registration's in the glove compartment.

Go ahead and open that up for me.

Mo did what he was told, and handed the documents over to the officer.

Do you know why I pulled you over today?

Mo knew his inspection was up-to-date, and he was fairly certain that his license plate was secure and visible, and that his lights were intact and functioning.

I must have been speeding, I guess...

Actually, no. I pulled you over because it is unlawful to use a turning lane for the purposes of passing a car on the right-hand through traffic lane.

I'm sorry, I had no idea...

Nobody ever does. What's your destination today?

Uh, to lunch. I'm meeting a friend for lunch.

In Princeton?

Princeton Junction.

Princeton Junction? There's no restaurants in Princeton Junction.

It's just a little Chinese place by the train station.

Ah, that's right. Happy Tails or whatever. Kung Pao dog meat and shit.

Yes sir.

Alright sir, I'll need you to wait right here inside your vehicle, and I'll be back with your documents in a few minutes.

Take it easy, man, just take it easy. It's only a moving violation. You'll get a ticket, and that'll be it. Just follow his instructions, answer his questions, and don't ask any yourself. Just keep breathing and keep cool. Mo could feel his cheeks getting hot, so he cranked the A/C up to max and angled the dashboard vents so they hit him directly in the face. Then he placed his hands firmly on the steering wheel and sat back in his seat to wait.

After a few minutes, the trooper exited his vehicle and strode back up to Mo's car. As he bent down to peer into the still-open driver's side window, Mo thought he noticed what he thought was a hint of sadism in those thin eyes, barely visible beneath the saucer-shaped hat.

This is not good.

Sir I noticed you shifting around a lot in your seat. Is there anything in your vehicle you're trying to hide from me? Any drugs or weapons or anything that might harm me? Anything I need to know about?

No sir. I apologize. I guess I didn't realize I was moving around...

I'm going to ask you to step out of the car now.

This is not good at all.

Mo thought about protesting, apologizing, denying... everything, really, but something in his soul was resigned to simply do what he was told, as if everything would be easier to endure that way, easier to survive. He opened his door and got out, and just as he did so, he noticed a second police car roll up behind the first one. The officer who emerged adjusted his belt beneath a staunch belly and swaggered his way up towards Mo and Officer Cerreta. There was still no hint of a breeze in the oppressive afternoon sun, but with this new officer's arrival, a distinct whiff of pre-ordained brutality came into the air.

Is this the suspect?

The suspect?

Yes. Sir, I'm going to ask you to walk back over to the other car with Officer McCluskey while I search your vehicle.

The suspect and the accused.

Stand right here, spread your feet, and put your hands on the side of the vehicle.

Mo acquiesced without protest. A few moments later, Officer Cerreta called out from the road ahead.

We got it, Lenny. The kid's not armed, but he's definitely packing something pretty hot here!

He was holding up Mo's jacket and the plastic sandwich bag containing exactly one ounce of pure, uncut cocaine.

The suspect, the accused, and the guilty.

Just then, the scanner in the cruiser crackled to life.

... NARCOTICS CENTRAL... THERE'S A BULLETIN... 10-69... PRINCETON JUNCTION...

The next thing he heard was Officer McCluskey's voice, ordering him to place his hands behind his back.

The station was located just a few miles away in Hamilton. The ride back there was not long; in fact, it was just long enough for Mo to wonder whether it was legal for officers to drive detainees around in the backs of their cars without fastening their seatbelts. The station itself was as imposing as a fortress, or some sort of compound, really, complete with a sub-station, a communications center, a maintenance garage, a firing range, and a helicopter pad. They pulled in to the facility, the tires giving a jubilant squeak on the brand new epoxy floor, and both officer Cerreta and officer McCluskey exited their cars and checked in at a window with the desk sergeant while Mo remained in the back seat. From that vantage point, he watched the mechanical comings-and-goings of an assortment of sergeants, troopers, and the occasional arrestee. After some time, Officer McCluskey returned to the car and opened the door.

Alright. Your turn now. Just walk with me. Straight ahead.

They walked down a hall, through a set of double swinging doors, and entered a small room. It was furnished more like an office than an interrogation room, though. After closing the door behind them, Officer McCluskey directed Mo to sit with a voice that a man might use to address a dog before assuming his own place behind the desk. After selecting a pen and arranging some documents in front of him, he began speaking to him without bothering to look him in the eye.

Name?

Guillermo, sir.

Your full name?

Guillermo Vicente Luna.

Have you ever been arrested before?

No sir.

Date of birth?

August second, 1977.

Residence?

Eighteen West 108th Street in Manhattan.

Officer McCluskey chuckled to himself for a moment, and then looked up at Mo for the first time since they entered the room. When he spoke again, it was in a pure, peremptory tone of voice.

You ain't in the old neighborhood now, are you?

No sir.

Officer McCluskey chuckled again and flipped through some of the remaining documents. Then, something on one of the pages happened to catch his eye.

You're a college student?

Yes sir.

Officer McCluskey leaned across his desk to get a better look at Mo's face before continuing.

Why on God's green earth would you play hell and get yourself into something like this?

I needed the money. *But no. This wasn't really about the money at all, was it? Every college kid could use a few extra G's every now and then. No. Of course that's not it. It's about failure. I failed at honesty, money, security, a degree, and when I anted up and kicked everything I had left into love, I failed at that too. After that, this was the only thing that seemed like something I could succeed at.*

Officer McCluskey just shook his head in disbelief. He slid a card half the size of a sheet of paper across the table towards Mo.

This is your Miranda card. You've been very cooperative so far, but you do need to affirm that you do have read and understand these rights...

It doesn't matter. I'll talk, I'll make a statement, I'll do whatever.

Officer McCluskey shook his head again.

Alright then. Here's your waver. Sign there at the bottom.

Mo began to speak, though his voice was so low, so meek, so insubstantial that it was very nearly drowned out by the breath of the air conditioning and the buzzing of the florescent lighting fixtures in the ceiling. He spoke as though he were some sort of automaton: he did not need to think, to remember, to formulate; he simply described the very recent past as if he were writing a short history book. It was so mechanical, in fact, that in the attic of his mind he was completely distant and distracted from the more pressing matters of his situation. There, in the tiny mouseholes of his memory where the past flits about in a vain attempt to escape amnesia, he thought of Marty. *At least she is above all this. Stronger than people like me. And without the need to be anything other than the simple, fractured person she was.*

Is there anything else you want to tell me?

No sir.

Alright then, Luna. In that case, it's time to go.

Unlike the rest of the facility, which was as technically advanced as a hospital, the detention area was a purely bare-bones affair. He and the officer walked beneath one final window, passed through a pair of heavy, slide-latching doors, and stepped into a world of cold lights, steel bars, and concrete. It was then that Mo began to see the other incarcerated faces, some watching staidly as he walked down the long hallway, some simply listening, heads down, to his footsteps while others watched with a predatory light in their eyes, and suddenly he was taken by a frenzied wrenching of the guts, felt his blood rushing into his ears, heard each heartbeat as loud and as clear as a pounding tympani, as he realized that this place was not filled with individual, monastic cells, but rather a series of larger, communal pens, and that he would probably, at some point in the very near future, have to fight with one of these watching and listening people. He clenched his fists so hard that his nails began to dig into his palms.

Stop here.

They were in front of one of the pens now, with only one other person inside. Officer McCluskey produced a ring of keys roughly the diameter of a coaster. As he selected the proper key for the lock, he spoke to the incumbent man.

Step back against the wall.

The man did as he was told.

Officer McCluskey unlocked the door.

Luna, you'll be staying here until an officer comes in to get you for processing.

How long does that take?

Officer McCluskey smirked.

Not exactly a veteran, are you, kid?

No sir.

Let's just say I'd make myself comfortable if I were you. If you have any other questions, just ask your new roommate here.

He grinned again, but Mo didn't see him. His head was hung in the physical language of defeat. When Officer McCluskey opened the door, it took all of his remaining strength simply to take the three steps needed to cross that threshold. He couldn't even turn around to watch as the door slammed shut behind him. When Officer McCluskey's footsteps had finally faded back down the long hallway, the other man in the pen spoke.

Yo, homes.

Mo didn't answer. The other man repeated himself, a bit more insistent this time.

Yo. Homes.

Mo looked up.

You didn't drink any of that coffee shit they have in there did you?

No.

That's good man, that's good. That's some toxic motherfucking coffee. Gives you the shits. And this is supposed to be a brand new facility, but the toilets in here don't work. They don't even have a Bern Bar.

He gestured towards the seatless, steel bowl that shared the pen with them.

Ain't that some shit.

Ain't that some shit is right. So wassup man? How'd you end up in this piece anyway?

Listen man, I don't feel much like talking.

Yeah, you're one of those "I'm innocent" motherfuckers. That's how it works. Everyone starts out believing they're innocent, believing that they don't deserve to be here. But after a week, they all start to realize that they're guilty, that they've always been guilty, and that they always will be. That's when everything starts to come apart.

Actually, I think I'm already there.

Damn homes, that's some cold ass shit for a young ass kid like you to be saying.

Yes, I've already reached that point. When these walls go up around you, all the other walls that made up your previous life start to crumble. They start to crumble, they start to fall, and they don't stop falling until a judge or parole board says they stop. Only then do you get to step out amidst the rubble to face it.

Mo had involuntarily (that is, naturally) assumed the universal posture of resignation, hunkered, stooped, bowed by the force of misery. He looked at one of the empty cots, and then to the other man for permission, who granted it with a shrug of the shoulders. Mo took a roll of toilet paper from the floor and, using it as a pillow, he lay down, turned his back to the wall, and closed his eyes. He wanted to find something—any memory, any story—that would take him away from this place, but the only thing he could think about was her. Marty. She was the crux of all of this, and for some time he thought that he might have to struggle to bear that crux the way Sisyphus bears his quotidian stone. But eventually something leapt into the light of his mind that pointed to a place almost foreign, alien even. *I told her I'd never been East of Jamaica. But I never told her about Montauk.*

After closing time one night at the Lion's Den, Dos Jotas was talking with Mo and a few other late night regulars about what it was like to go fishing off Montauk. It was something he did rather regularly during the summers, and as a result, he was a very well-informed raconteur. He talked about the time he drove his Criss Craft deep into a sand bar off Wills Point, not far from the eastern edge of Fort Pond Bay, and how he had to spend the entire day waiting for high water before he could wedge the vessel off the spit. Once he was free, and his itinerary changed, he decided to continue on through the dying light in a push to make it around the southern fluke of the whale's fin that is the Eastern tip of Long Island. An hour later, under a waxing moon, the bioluminescent plankton began to glow all around his hull, drawing a school of baitfish. As the baitfish began to feed, squid rose up from the depths to feast madly upon them, and this frenzy went on for another hour or so as he scudded across the ink-black water. Suddenly, just off his lee bow, a blue shark materialized. It was a monster, he said, meaning it was perhaps ten feet in length, not that it was some sort of grotesque, fisherman's beast. In fact, rather than casting a line (he'd gone shark fishing many times before, and said that a mako especially will fight like hell on the hook), he found himself mesmerized by its beauty. It veritably soared through the water on incredibly long, tapered pectorals, and the water was so packed with squid that it didn't even have to hunt; rather, it could lethargically open its maw from time to time and a squid would simply fall inside. Nearer the dawn, the phosphorescence began to wink out, the squid returned to the abyss, and the monster blue returned to his pelagic ways. As first light began to break across the eastern horizon, he heard the tolling of a buoy signifying the nearness of the shore. He cruised back across the morning waters, past the rotting pilings, past the tallgrass dunes flecked with the large pink blossoms of the rose mallow, past the commercial fishermen mending their nets as they lay across their laps like a shawl, all the way back to the dock.

As Mo lay there on his cot, imagining the waters that lay off Montauk, he found peace in the realization that the sea has no memory. The wake of even the largest oceangoing vessel is quickly and unequivocally erased. Memory will persist, even when the surface of the water has been swept clear, but it does so only in the flesh. And for as long as he would need to, he could lay on that unforgiving cot and remember once having listened to a story about spending a night alone at sea. He would lie there in this womb, this space devoid of all things sinful or hopeful, enduring the boredom, the fretful hours, the acquired patterns, waiting for the day when he would be born again, new to the world, no longer forced to heave a boulder of guilt up the side of a mountain.

No. Sisyphus may never be happy, but he may always remember, and perhaps that will be enough.◆

The Lantern

A S OFFICERS COFFEY AND SCAGNETTI escorted him into the 77th Precinct, Willie couldn't help but think that the building itself, whose cinder block walls were painted with several coats of neutral white paint, looked like it had been a public high school in a previous life before being reincarnated as a squad house. He was processed by a young man, younger than himself, certainly, and probably fresh out of the academy, though he wore the haughty expression of someone who had just graduated Phi Beta Kappa from some Ivy League school. There was a lazy, almost contemptuous look in his eyes, and the fact that he now had to look up from that morning's New York Post and deal with the arresting officers only added to the sense of scorn.

What'd you bring me now?

Officer Scagnetti spoke.

Just read the report. Should be self-explanatory. He walked out on his shift at work, boss phoned it in to the parole board, and when we responded, we found him in a neighbor's apartment with a marijuana pipe containing a small amount of residue.

After his partner provided the formalities, Officer Coffey added an editorial.

Junkies just don't have any sense. They behave themselves on the inside so they can get released, and once they're free, they start acting the fool all over again.

Just like Helen Keller. No sense.

The three laughed. Then the processing officer spoke.

Well, he's a parole violator, so we know he's already in the system. Just put him in the holding pen and we'll deal with him later. I'm hungry. Let's get a taco.

Sounds good to me.

God damn right it sounds good. So put José here in the pen already and let's go.

The holding pen was aptly named; if anything, it was more of a cage. Three sets of steel bars backed up against one of the cinder block walls. Officer Coffey took the keys from a lockbox and unlatched the sliding door.

In you go...

Willie walked in, stoic and resigned. He stood there, in the middle of the pen, while Officer Coffey slammed the door shut behind him with a sudden, frenzied clash. He kept his back turned until he could no longer hear footsteps falling on the vinyl floor of the hallway. Finally, he turned around, and grasped the bars of the pen in the way that condemned men are wont to do. After a few minutes, when the cold steel began to warm in his grip and his palms began to sweat, he would shift a step or two to the left or the right and adjust his hands. He spent the next couple of hours doing that, exactly that, and nothing but that, so help him God. *This is all too familiar. Different state, different cops, same old clink. William Faulkner once wrote that the past is never dead. But now I know it's not alive, either. Not really, anyway. It's a thin, tenuous ghost unable to do anything but reach out for you. Like a distant spring, enduring and unrecoverable no matter what the yearning, buried though alive. It's not festering. It's rotting. When something festers, it swells, it flares up. But when something rots, all it leaves is a void. And that's all this is. An oubliette. A place for putting people away to rot...*

Some time later that afternoon, a different officer approached the holding pen with a different suspect in custody. Before he put key to lock, he barked sharply at Willie.

Step back from the bars.

Willie complied silently, the officer slid open the door, and the new man entered. When the door clanged home again, the man looked at Willie and smiled. His teeth were so rotten that it looked like he had a mouthful of dominos, and his eyes were half shaded, half obscured by thick, matted dreadlocks. Willie nodded at him but did not smile.

I's Jerusalem Hayes, my friend! What your name be?

Willie was disinclined to answer. There are two kinds of people in the world: people who say, "Do you know me?" when they meet a stranger, and people who say, "Do I know you?" He had learned that, in prison, it's most often the former. But there was something in this man's nasty grin that belied a deeper current of honesty and kindness, and he decided to answer.

Willie.

Ah, it be Willie den. How long you been set to linger in dis jungle here?

Don't know. Few hours, maybe.

Soon dey be taking you to the Tombs. In dat place they be glad to hang ya. Yes boy. You can be no semi-contender in dere.

You're telling me.

Yes boy! You no retreat, you no surrender. Tings blow up quick like gasoline! I be on da street corner with me tampee when de police man pull up! Now I be caught in here like a rat in a blender, yes boy!

Legalize it.

Jerusalem Hayes flashed his broad, domino smile again, and laughed uproariously.

Dis be what I's been saying! See you understand. Now my brother, you tell me dis... how long it's been since you had youself a woman?

Willie had thought about that himself recently. And now that he had been asked, he remembered: it was the night he'd gotten coked up at a party with a bunch of fashionable strangers. But the actual woman wasn't one of them. No; he had known her. He had known her quite well, as a matter of fact. *We had made a plan together. The kind of plan that men and women make when they believe they're about spend the rest of their lives together; the kind of plan that I never expected would happen before I met her. She liked swimming, and she wanted to buy a home and move up into the Hudson Valley. She liked jewelry, too. Necklaces and bracelets, mostly. But I'll never speak to her again. If anything, I'll send her a postcard from the precinct here, with the message "This is where we're honeymooning at."*

As soon as that realization crept back into his mind, the entire vision fled from his thoughts with a sickening revulsion. *I don't even care about going without sex. It's having no contact with society that's rough. It was simple, basic routine and endurance that got me through my original sentence, but when they slap me with another two to four for violating parole... that's when things will start to get difficult. I don't know if I have enough left to keep my mind occupied for that much time...*

No, dis be no place for the flesh, boy. Dis be a place for song!

Jerusalem Hayes whooped and crowed with laughter. When the spell passed, he began to bop up and down, swaying from side to side as he sang:

> By the rivers of Babylon
> Where he sat down
> And there he wept when he remembered Zion.
> Oh from wicked, carry us away from captivity
> Required from us a song
> How can we sing King Alpha's song in a strange land ...

Willie never made it to the Tombs. After another couple of hours, a spot opened up on a judge's calendar, and an officer arrived to take him to court. As he sat him down in the back of the patrol car, he informed Willie that someone from the Legal Aid Society would be there to represent him. As a caveat, he added,

Not that it'll matter much, anyway. I read the report.

Willie expected that would be the case. But when he was delivered to the courthouse, his public defender had some surprising news for him.

We have a character witness who has offered to testify on your behalf...

A character witness? Who could that be?

A New Jersey State Police officer named Gino Libretti.

Libretti's going to vouch for me?

And I don't want to get your hopes up, but there's another development that might work in our favor.

What are you talking about?

The woman whose apartment you were arrested in has given a statement to police attesting to the fact that the pipe you were found with actually belongs to her. She's facing one count of simple possession of drug paraphernalia, but it takes the focus off of you.

Alba Lucía is involved with this too...

Willie and his council had about an hour to prepare their case. Willie used the majority of that time not to explain or defend himself, but simply to tell his story. After his attorney relayed his version of that story to the court, the sitting judge called the court into recess while he retired to his antechamber to reach a decision. When he called the court back into session a half hour later, he addressed Willie in a measured, dispassionate voice.

In the case between the People of the State of New York versus Guillermo Vicente Luna, we essentially have but one question to answer here today: does merely signing a parole or probation agreement constitute consent to an unwarranted search? Or, must consent be given at the time of the search in question, because such a document is merely an agreement to consent when the question arises about whether or not they should allow a search. Presumably, a parolee or probationer would be in violation—and thereby have their parole/probation revoked—if they elect not to consent to an unwarranted search, simply by not giving the consent they already agreed to give. However, this court believes it is necessary under the law to differentiate the authority to conduct a "home visit" from the authority to conduct a "search." I have researched statutory language and have come to the determination that the authority to conduct a home visit and the authority to conduct a search were found in different sections of the penal statute. Therefore, one that was authorized to conduct a home visit could not be automatically deemed authorized to conduct a home search. Thus, it is the ruling of this court that Fourth Amendment protection extends to all persons, whether on parole or not. The officers of the 77th Precinct were not authorized to conduct a search of the probationer's home and property. That, coupled with the testimony of a long-serving officer of the law, and with a plea agreement made by a second defendant, it is the decision of this court that the defendant is to be released from custody in good order and returned to his probationary status forthwith.

The judge brought his gavel down, cracking it like a whip, and with that, Willie was free to go. He shook hands with his public defender, thanking him vigorously for everything he'd done in his short amount of time. Then, he turned to face the gallery, searching for Alba Lucía. When he finally made his way over to her, they embraced.

I can't believe you're here ... But why did you do this? What did they give you for copping to the possession charge?

Al's eyes glowed as warm and welcoming as a bouquet of flowers left on your doorstep.

You should know. I got probation, of course! Like that matters anyway, since I'm already living on borrowed time, right?

They both smiled, filled with a carefree sense of blithe relief. It was late in the morning, but Willie felt as if the light of the four holy stars was breaking all around him; as if some lantern had just lead him out from the depths of night that keep the hellish valley in eternal darkness; as if the laws of the abyss had been broken, allowing him, though damned, to step out onto the concrete streets of the city once again. *In the end, that's all life really is... probation,* he thought to himself. But the only thought he could actually verbalize at the moment was something quite different indeed.

Well, shit! ◆

Acknowledgements

I WOULD LIKE TO POSTHUMOUSLY thank my advisor at Princeton, Professor Robert Fagles. Borges once suggested that when writers die, they become books. To that, I would like to add the notion that all books—whether written, read, translated, or reincarnated—are an odyssey. I am ever grateful to have been a very small part of his.

Thanks also to Gregory Rabassa, writer, teacher, raconteur, friend.

To the Banff Centre, for their generosity, their hospitality, and for enabling art in all its myriad forms.

To Gabrielle David, Vagabond Beaumont, and Kevin E. Tobar Pesántez, for bringing this to fruition.

To Tim Brown, Jeanette Holland, Terry Bennett, Teri Wood, Vickie Smith, Lee Boyd, Linda Ramieh, Jeanne Pride, Phil Jones, Hal Wilson, Dana Allen, Karen Kronenberg, and Beppe Gualino, who died before having a chance to read this book.

To Felice Apolinski, Amy Prichard, Lisa Davis, Dick Boland, Josh Griffith, and Karen Johnson, for the Monday mornings.

To Keith Wallman, for the Brooklyn days.

To Craig Baruk and Seth Fabian, for the uptown nights.

To Alberto Fuguet and Eloy Urroz, for leading by example.

And to Alba, who is my morning light.◆

About the Author

EZRA E. FITZ began his literary life at Princeton University, studying under the tutelage of James Irby, C.K. Williams, and Jonathan Galassi. He has worked with Grammy winning musician Juanes, Emmy winning journalist Jorge Ramos, and the king of soccer himself, Pelé. His translations of contemporary Latin American literature by Alberto Fuguet and Eloy Urroz have been praised by *The New York Times, The Washington Post, The New Yorker,* and *The Believer,* among other publications. His work has appeared in *The Boston Review, Harper's Magazine,* and *Words Without Borders,* and he was a 2010 Resident at the Banff International Literary Translation Centre in Alberta, Canada. THE MORNING SIDE OF THE HILL is Fitz' first novella. www.ezrafitz.com.◆

Sinclair Lewis is yours, and as such, interesting and important to us.
William Faulkner is both yours and ours, and as such, essential to us.

—Carlos Fuentes

OTHER BOOKS BY 2LEAF PRESS

2LEAF PRESS challenges the status quo by publishing alternative fiction, non-fiction, poetry and bilingual works by activists, academics, poets and authors dedicated to diversity and social justice with scholarship that is accessible to the general public. 2LEAF PRESS produces high quality and beautifully produced hardcover, paperback and ebook formats through our series: *2LP Explorations in Diversity, 2LP University Books, 2LP Classics, 2LP Translations, Nuyorican World Series,* and *2LP Current Affairs, Culture & Politics.* Below is a selection of 2LEAF PRESS' published titles.

2LP EXPLORATIONS IN DIVERSITY
Substance of Fire: Gender and Race in the College Classroom
by Claire Millikin
Foreword by R. Joseph Rodríguez, Afterword by Richard Delgado
Contributed material by Riley Blanks, Blake Calhoun, Rox Trujillo

Black Lives Have Always Mattered
A Collection of Essays, Poems, and Personal Narratives
Edited by Abiodun Oyewole

The Beiging of America:
Personal Narratives about Being Mixed Race in the 21st Century
Edited by Cathy J. Schlund-Vials, Sean Frederick Forbes, Tara Betts
with an Afterword by Heidi Durrow

What Does it Mean to be White in America?
Breaking the White Code of Silence, A Collection of Personal Narratives
Edited by Gabrielle David and Sean Frederick Forbes
Introduction by Debby Irving and Afterword by Tara Betts

2LP UNIVERSITY BOOKS
Designs of Blackness, Mappings in the Literature and
Culture of African Americans
A. Robert Lee
20TH ANNIVERSARY EXPANDED EDITION

2LP CLASSICS
Adventures in Black and White
Edited and with a critical introduction by Tara Betts
by Philippa Duke Schuyler

Monsters: Mary Shelley's Frankenstein and Mathilda
by Mary Shelley, edited by Claire Millikin Raymond

2LP TRANSLATIONS
Birds on the Kiswar Tree
by Odi Gonzales, Translated by Lynn Levin
Bilingual: English/Spanish

Incessant Beauty, A Bilingual Anthology
by Ana Rossetti, Edited and Translated by Carmela Ferradáns
Bilingual: English/Spanish

NUYORICAN WORLD SERIES
Our Nuyorican Thing, The Birth of a Self-Made Identity
by Samuel Carrion Diaz, with an Introduction by Urayoán Noel
Bilingual: English/Spanish

Hey Yo! Yo Soy!, 40 Years of Nuyorican Street Poetry,
The Collected Works of Jesús Papoleto Meléndez
Bilingual: English/Spanish

LITERARY NONFICTION
No Vacancy; Homeless Women in Paradise
by Michael Reid

The Beauty of Being, A Collection of Fables, Short Stories & Essays
by Abiodun Oyewole

WHEREABOUTS: Stepping Out of Place,
An Outside in Literary & Travel Magazine Anthology
Edited by Brandi Dawn Henderson

PLAYS
Rivers of Women, The Play
by Shirley Bradley LeFlore, with photographs by Michael J. Bracey

AUTOBIOGRAPHIES/MEMOIRS/BIOGRAPHIES
Trailblazers, Black Women Who Helped Make America Great
American Firsts/American Icons
by Gabrielle David

Mother of Orphans
The True and Curious Story of Irish Alice, A Colored Man's Widow
by Dedria Humphries Barker

Strength of Soul
by Naomi Raquel Enright

Dream of the Water Children:
Memory and Mourning in the Black Pacific
by Fredrick D. Kakinami Cloyd
Foreword by Velina Hasu Houston, Introduction by Gerald Horne
Edited by Karen Chau

The Fourth Moment: Journeys from the Known to the Unknown, A Memoir
by Carole J. Garrison, Introduction by Sarah Willis

POETRY
PAPOLíTICO, Poems of a Political Persuasion
by Jesús Papoleto Meléndez
with an Introduction by Joel Kovel and DeeDee Halleck

Critics of Mystery Marvel, Collected Poems
by Youssef Alaoui, with an Introduction by Laila Halaby

shrimp
by jason vasser-elong, with an Introduction by Michael Castro
The Revlon Slough, New and Selected Poems
by Ray DiZazzo, with an Introduction by Claire Millikin

Written Eye: Visuals/Verse
by A. Robert Lee

A Country Without Borders: Poems and Stories of Kashmir
by Lalita Pandit Hogan, with an Introduction by Frederick Luis Aldama

Branches of the Tree of Life
The Collected Poems of Abiodun Oyewole 1969-2013
by Abiodun Oyewole, edited by Gabrielle David
with an Introduction by Betty J. Dopson

2Leaf Press is an imprint owned and operated by the Intercultural Alliance of Artists & Scholars, Inc. (IAAS), a NY-based nonprofit organization that publishes and promotes multicultural literature.

NEW YORK
www.2leafpress.org